All or Nothing

The Sequel
To
Serigala Valley

Written by Haley Langwood

Cover Art by Haley Langwood

This is a work of fiction. The places, names, characters, businesses, and incidents are the author's imagination. Any kind of resemblance to persons dead or alive is a coincidence.

Table of Contents

Chapter 01

"Russia? They are in Russia? Fuck, no!" I yelled in frustration. Lamar sighed; he didn't look too happy either, I could tell, but he appeared much calmer than me. "Arkady is on his way to Rublyovka as we speak," my father said, and he spoke in a low, soothing voice. I knew why he used his calming, reassuring tone. My father was afraid that I would lose control over my tiger, again. I understood because it was something that I needed to work on.

My father had explained that my tiger was extremely strong, and because I only had started shifting recently, my tiger had gained even more power, willpower, that is. And because I still wasn't able to completely control my tiger, he sometimes took control. When my tiger broke free, it mostly ended in disaster because I couldn't stop him. The only one able to stop my tiger was the doctor, and only because he used a particular medication to subdue my tiger.

Grandma Natalya Balashov, and Grandma Anichka Vasiliev, were teaching me how to meditate. Control the mind, control the tiger, they had told me.

No one had expected that Igor and Liam would flee to Russia of all places. Yet, it had been logical for Igor to seek protection in Rublyovka because many family members were still living there. My father had once explained that Rublyovka is a suburb of Moscow; it was where I was born. My family had lived there for many years.

Could it be that more of my family members were involved? It was evident that Igor wanted me out of the way. He had used one of my best friends to get close enough so that he could poison me. First, he had used the family he had paid to take me in, to feed me the herbs that would prevent my tiger from surfacing. God only knows what he had told them where the herbs were for. The man was a nutcase but a dangerous nutcase.

Later, when I moved to Serigala Valley, he had used Liam, who was supposed to be my friend. Liam had mixed the poison into the moisturizer, which was created especially for me. For more than twenty-six years, Igor had controlled my life because he had managed to keep my tiger subdued—the rat bastard.

Eight months had passed since we found out that Liam, one of my best friends, had betrayed me. We now were sure that Igor had been the mastermind behind it all. What I didn't understand was why Liam had betrayed me. I really needed an answer to that question. Then, there was the question of how many family members and friends were in cahoots with Igor?

Could my mother be in Rublyovka, as well? I hoped not, but if she were, then I would travel to Russia. I was determined to find her because she was my mother. It was time to bring her home, where she belonged. And no one would stop me, no one!

"When did he leave? For Rublyovka, I mean," I inquired. "A couple of hours ago," my father replied. I nodded. I couldn't wait to hear from Arkady, and I prayed that he would be able to locate Igor and Liam.

Grandmother Natalya was still teaching me new spells and how to make all kinds of different potions. She was happy and so proud that I turned out to be a natural when it came to casting spells. "One day, you will become a powerful wizard, and that will make you an even more powerful tiger shifter," she had said after I successfully cast a highly complex spell. Grandma Natalya was proud of me, which made me feel ten feet tall. However, I still had difficulties brewing potions, but I hoped I'd also manage that in time.

I now knew how to make Liam talk because I knew a spell to get him to spill the beans. To make him talk, we had to find him first. For the last eight months, Igor had been successful in hiding. Now, our people in Russia had spotted Igor where we didn't expect him. It appeared that all this time, he had hidden in plain sight. Un-fucking-believable. I must admit that Igor had nerves, and since everyone had told me that the shifter wasn't afraid of my father, it didn't make sense that he was on the run.

If Igor really wasn't afraid of facing Alexei Balashov's wrath, then he should have stayed and fight. However, Igor chose to flee to Russia, hoping to be safe, well, how wrong he was. We would get him because, in the end, there would be no place to hide for him and Liam.

It still was difficult to comprehend that Igor had fled to Russia, to Rublyovka of all places. That didn't make sense because it was where many family members were still living. They knew what was going on and that Igor was a bastard who had deceived Alexei in the most horrific way—letting the man believe that his mate and newborn son were dead? Who would do something like that?

Anyway, that was how we knew where he was hiding. I suspected that at least a couple of family members were in cahoots with Igor. However, most of them were on our side, which felt good. I wondered if I was permitted to travel to Russia to help search for Igor and Liam.

"We will remain here, sweetheart," Lamar whispered in my ear, making me shiver. He chuckled. "I love it that I have such an effect on you, my mate," he admitted. "I will always love you and want you. That will never change," I promised. "I know, sweetheart," Lamar said as he kissed me on the top of my head.

Milo came to stand in front of us, wagging his tail, and then he started barking. "That's my cue to get some fresh air," I said. "No, you stay here with my father. I won't be long," I assured my mate when he wanted to go with me.

Lamar wasn't happy, but I needed some alone time. Ever since we knew about Liam and Igor, I had a bodyguard surrounding me where ever I went. It was either Arkady, Lamar, my father, or one of Lamar's betas. "I won't leave the premises," I promised. Lamar still didn't look happy, but he kept his tongue.

I glanced at Lamar and then at my father, who looked, well, proud. I let my gaze rest on Lamar. "Besides, I have the best bodyguard I could wish for at my side," I grinned. My father nodded in approval; Lamar still didn't look happy. Milo wasn't a fighter; in fact, he was a cuddle bear. However, should someone try to harm me, then my cuddle bear wasn't so cuddly anymore. Then he acted like the powerful dog that he was.

I had never before seen my dog aggressive until hyena shifters attacked me; Milo had come through fighting three of the damn beasts simultaneously. One hyena had wounded Milo by tearing into my dog's hind leg. Milo hadn't budged and had killed the second hyena by tearing his throat out. I was shocked and proud at the same time.

I took Milo to the small forest that was still on the premises. My dog loved roaming the woods. I went to the pond and sat down on a log near the water. I thought about Liam and his betrayal. It still was surreal and hard to accept that Liam, of all people, was the one who had poisoned me. Did he know that I was a shifter? Or had Igor lied to him about the effect of the herbs? So many questions and no answers drove me mad.

I don't know how long I had been sitting near the waterfront, but the ringing of my phone had me look away from the water. It was Lamar, and it was now that I realized that it was dark, shit.

"Hey Lamar," I greeted my mate, and I tried to sound casual but couldn't pull it off. "Mitchell, where are you? Are you alright?" Lamar sounded almost frantic. I told him where I was, and he told me to stay put, that he would come and get me. Then he ended the call. Milo sat next to me, and he was on high alert. "Milo? What's wrong, boy?" I asked my dog. And yes, I knew that I wouldn't get an answer because dogs can't talk.

I could tell that something was wrong, though, because Milo was staring straight forward. Something or someone had Milo on high alert, which wasn't good. Still, it didn't seem likely because the premises should be safe. The house wasn't even that far.

"Milo? Boy?" I said, but the dog kept staring straight ahead. "Mitchell? Thank God that you're alright," Lamar said as he hugged the life out of me. "I'm sorry that I made you worry, but I forgot the time. Is something wrong?" I said.

"There are hyenas in the area because the alarm went off, which means that they could be on the premises. So we need to get inside," Lamar urged.

The moment Lamar spoke the words, the growls started, and I saw four hyenas running toward us. I called for Milo to stay put, but the dog ran directly towards the hyenas. He wanted to defend and kill; I felt it, which was weird. I actually felt the hatred my dog felt for the hyenas. Well, now was not the time to analyze that phenomenon.

Lamar changed into his wolf, and within seconds, I changed into my second tiger form without even thinking. The change came so suddenly that I shook my head to clear my mind, then the fight was on. Two hyenas were fighting Milo, my dog was strong and could hold his own, but he was losing when two more hyenas jumped him from behind. Now there were six of the damn beast, shit.

I looked at my mate and saw that he was fighting two hyenas. He should be able to take both beasts down, so I ran toward Milo. I grabbed the hyena that was clawing Milo's back. I grabbed him by the neck and pulled him off my dog. "You attacked my dog, big mistake," I said as I looked the hyena in its eyes right before I snapped its neck.

I threw the dead hyena aside and grabbed the second one when I felt pain. Shit, one of the beasts was tearing my back open. I roared in a fury; then, the weight was lifted. I turned and saw that my father snapped the beast's neck that had been on my back a minute ago. I turned and snapped the hyena's neck that still was in my grip.

Milo had ripped out the throat of one hyena and was fighting the last of the four beasts. I wanted to help him, but my father stopped me; he still was in his tiger form and thus, couldn't speak. Nevertheless, I understood and let my dog handle the last beast.

Lamar had killed the two hyenas that had attacked him, and Milo had ended the last hyena's life. My dog came to stand beside me, his massive head against my thigh. I was amazed at seeing so much hatred in the beast's eyes.

Chapter 02

"Just stir two times to the left and one to the right, then it should be ready," Grandma Natalya Balashov instructed. I did as I was told and smiled when the potion I was brewing changed from a light yellow to a dark purple. Yep, it was ready.

I smiled because I had just finished my first healing potion. "You're getting better with each potion that you make, Kotyonok," said Grandma Natalya. I could tell that she was proud of me, which made me ten feet tall.

My grandmother made me study her book with recipes for many different potions. "I really need to walk, Milo," I told my grandmother. She nodded, "Don't go too far," she cautioned. "I won't, but Milo and I need to get some fresh air. Besides, no shifter would attack in the middle of the day," I replied, smiling.

Grandma Natalya didn't smile; she looked worried. "Promise me that you listen to your tiger. If it senses danger, then you would come home immediately," she urged. I promised that I would, then I leashed Milo and left.

I decided to stay near the premises because Grandma Natalya was right; it was too dangerous. By now, I was a powerful tiger, and I certainly could hold my own. However, if five or so hyenas would attack, then I would be in trouble, big time.

When I reached the dirt road, I unleashed Milo, and the dog took off immediately. Milo liked to run. "Milo? Milo?" I called when he disappeared into the bushes. Nothing, no Milo, so I began to panic. Milo didn't run away, and when I called him, he always responded. Either he barked, or he came running back to me. I didn't hear him bark this time, and he didn't come running back, either.

Suddenly I heard Milo growl, which was never a good sign. I sprinted to where Milo had disappeared, and that's when I saw three men trying to take Milo. Well, that wouldn't do; no one hurt my dog and got away with it. "Hey, let my dog go," I growled. They needed to split, which would mean that Milo stood a chance to defend himself.

Then I saw that they had managed to get a rope around Milo's neck; they would be able to strangle him. That's when I saw red, and my tiger fought to get out. It wanted to tear out the throats of the thugs who tried to take Milo. I managed to keep the upper hand and not shift, but it wasn't easy.

Two men came toward me, which was a huge mistake because Milo immediately attacked the one man that was holding the rope. I took the first idiot down by putting my fist against his throat. My roundhouse kick surprised the second idiot; he went down as well. I glanced at Milo and saw that he had his assailant on the ground, his massive jaws clamped around the man's throat. I took my phone and called Lamar.

Within minutes I saw Lamar running toward me, and with him was Grandma Natalya and Grandma Anichka Gurkovsky Vasiliev. Both women looked from me to the three men lying on the ground. Milo was standing above them, growling menacingly.

Grandma Anichka looked intently at me with her deep green eyes, eyes so much like mine. "What happened? Who are these men?" she asked. I shrugged and told her that I didn't know who they were. I did know, however, that these three idiots weren't shifters; they were human.

"I can search their minds for answers," Grandma Natalya offered. I frowned because I didn't know that something like that was possible. "Does it damage their brains?" I questioned. Grandma Natalya shook her head. "No," she replied. "I can alter their minds if you're finished with them," Grandma Anichka said, looking expectantly at Grandma Natalya.

******

"I can't believe it. These criminals wanted Milo so they could use him as a fighting dog?" I felt the rage rise again. After Grandma Natalya had invaded their minds and retrieved the information, I had been beside myself with fury. My tiger wanted out, and I had let him because I was too tired to hold him back any longer. Yep, I still wasn't able to control my tiger. I, or rather my tiger, had killed all three men. People who let dogs fight each other for money are monsters, not humans. So, I didn't consider it murder.

I read that people who organize these dog fights steal dogs from their owners. Also, they breed their own fight dogs, and these dogs live in appalling conditions. They are used and abused in the most horrific ways that most people can't even imagine. These scumbags used even small dogs for the fighting dogs to tear apart. If it were up to me, I would kill each and every monster who is involved in dogfighting. Thank God I could save Milo from such a terrible fate; the thought alone made me shiver.

Grandma Natalya had retrieved more information from the three men. So now, we had eight names from the monsters who let the poor dogs fight each other. Lamar promised me that they would get what they deserved, which satisfied me to no end.

I calmed down and sipped from my tea when my phone began to ring. I knew that particular tone; it was the salon.

"I need to go to the salon because Mason has come down with the flu," I informed my mate. "I go with you because you're still in danger with Igor on the loose and the hyenas," Lamar said, and he sounded pretty adamant.

I shook my head. "No, I can hold my own. I'm not helpless. Plus, I need some normalcy again. Everyone is guarding me, and it drives me crazy," I insisted. Lamar didn't look happy, but I wouldn't back down, not this time. I was Lamar's mate, his equal, and still, he treated me as if I was weak and helpless. Frankly, I was done with people who ruled my life.

"Baby, you can't go without at least one bodyguard," Lamar said in a soothing tone. That tone made me even more determined to go alone without extra protection. I had my tiger and my dog; that was all I needed. It was a relief that Lamar finally relented.

I took Milo with me as I headed for my car. I was shocked when I entered the salon. "Jesus, you look like death warmed over," I said when I stepped into my office and saw a very sick Jason. "Thank you, charming as ever,"

Jason replied after he blew his nose and had a coughing fit. "Let me take you home," I said because there was no way that I would let my manager behind the wheel. Jason really was in a terrible state.

By the time I was back, the salon was packed. "Thank God that you're back," said Christine. I started immediately with my first customer, Mrs. Johnson. She wasn't an easy woman to please, but I knew how to handle her.

It was about an hour later when suddenly my tiger reacted strangely. It was like he scented someone familiar, someone important to us. My tiger wanted to leave the salon because it knew that my dear mate, Lamar was near. Goddamn, he was guarding me, even after I told him specifically not to do so. Why didn't he listen to me? He never listened to what I wanted, what I needed.

My last customer had left, and I was exhausted. My tiger was restless, and I knew why. Lamar was still in the neighborhood. Damn him! I leashed Milo, closed and locked the door. "Lamar, you can show yourself; I know that you're close," I growled.

"Hey, baby. Is everything alright? You sound so tense," Lamar said as he emerged from the shadows. I sighed because I didn't want to fight with my mate, but he had to learn to respect my wishes. "Lamar, I appreciate that you are concerned for my safety. But, you, following me around, has to stop. It's driving me mad, and I really need some kind of normalcy. So, please, please, stop following me. I call you or my father when I need help. I trust my tiger to warn me if danger lies ahead," I insisted.

Well, if I had expected that Lamar would apologize and leave, I was badly mistaken. "Baby, I will always look out for you because you're my mate. You are precious, and I don't want to see you hurt. So, you better get used to me, or one of the pack, watching over you," Lamar said.

After hearing his words, I don't know where the rage I felt came from, but it was there. "Yeah, well, you know what? Just leave and let me do things the way I want to. Mate or not, I need time away from you. Just go," I growled as I moved away from Lamar.

"Baby? What are you talking about? You're my mate; we belong together. Let me protect you. Mitchell, you need my protection," Lamar's voice rose with every word that he spoke. I wasn't impressed. No, if anything, I was fed up; I was done with everyone who didn't listen to what I wanted. Lamar was my mate, but I needed to get away from him right now. The man was smothering me slowly, and he wasn't even aware that he was doing it.

"You can't leave, Mitchell! Mitchell," Lamar yelled after me. I ignored him as I opened the backdoor for Milo to jump onto the backseat. Then, I climbed behind the wheel of my vehicle. I slammed the door close and drove off like a bat out of hell. To my relief, I didn't see him following me. No headlights behind me, good!

After I calmed down enough to think things through, I realized that I didn't want to go back to the house Lamar and I shared. I didn't want to go to my father's place either. I knew that it was the first place Lamar would search for me.

I turned the car and drove back to the salon because I still had the apartment above The Cutting Edge Hair Salon.

Chapter 03

I woke in confusion because this wasn't our bedroom. Shit, I was in my bedroom in my apartment above the salon. Lamar and I had a massive fallout the previous evening. I wondered if he would ever talk to me again. Then again, I really needed some normalcy in my life. Ever since I found out about being a tiger shifter, my life had turned upside down.

I felt like I didn't have time to breathe, to summarize everything that had happened to me. I had fought hyenas and rogue tiger shifters. My tiger even had gotten the upper hand, and I had disappeared for months. My best friend had tried to poison me, and my Great Uncle Igor had deprived me of growing up with my birth parents. Plus, my great uncle wanted me dead, and God only knew why.

Now, I carried my father's last name, which was my birthright. I was now officially a Balashov. If that wasn't enough, I wasn't only a tiger shifter; no, it turned out that I was a witch as well. Now, my grandmother was teaching me how to brew potions and cast spells. My father once told me that I didn't react normally to all the changes that had happened in a short amount of time.

I drank my morning coffee, fed Milo, and then I took him to the park. I needed to get to the salon in time because Mason was sick. Milo was in my office, and I unlocked the door so the customers could enter. Christine, Raoul, and Jennifer were already preparing for the first customers.

"I'll be in my office," I said when my phone started to ring. It was my father, and he wanted to know what had happened the previous night. I reluctantly told him of the outburst I had. "Yes, Lamar told me about that," my father said. I frowned because, what the hell. "Did you discuss me? I mean, father, with all due respect, that is something between Lamar and me," I said, as I tried to keep my tone neutral.

"I wanted to see you this morning, so I came by the house. Lamar looked awful, and I sensed that something was wrong. So, I asked, and he told me what had happened, my father explained. Lamar shouldn't have done that because this was between my mate and me. "Are you planning on going home after work?" my father inquired.

I sighed because it didn't matter how angry I had been; I missed my mate. "I guess so," I softly replied. "Good, because running away is never the answer. You two need to talk. You need to work out whatever problems you have," my father said, and he sounded strange, emotional.

"I know, dad. I will talk to Lamar, but." I stopped because I didn't exactly know what to say. "I'll see you and Lamar at my place because your Grandma Natalya is going to cook," my father said, and he sounded his old self again. I wondered why he had sounded so emotional.

"Jennifer, could you close up for me? I need to go home," I said. Jennifer, of course, told me to go, and she would close the salon. It wasn't the first time that she helped me out like that. I thanked her, leashed Milo, and went to my car.

I frowned when I drove up to the house and didn't see Lamar's vehicle. I checked the garage, but it was empty.

Could it be that my mate was at the police station? I took my phone and hit speed dial. Lamar answered on the first ring. "Hey," he said. My mate sounded cautious, and I didn't like that one bit.

"Hey. How are you?" I asked because I didn't really know what to say. "I'm okay, but I would feel better if you were in my arms," Lamar softly replied. I sighed because I felt the same way. "I feel the same way. I miss you, babe," I whispered hoarsely. "Where are you now," Lamar asked. "I'm home, or, in front of our home. I thought that you would be there." I paused, then I said, "We need to talk." Lamar agreed, but he was called to a crime scene, so I would have to wait until he returned. "I'll be here," I promised. "I love you so much," Lamar whispered, making me shiver with need. I had spent the night without my mate, and I hadn't liked it. "I love you too, babe," I returned.

It was nearly midnight when Lamar finally returned home. I had been worried, but I knew that if he was on a case, then it could take a while before he got home. The moment Lamar came through the door, I flew into his arms and started kissing him. My tongue was probing his lips, demanding access to his hot, wet mouth.

Lamar parted his lips immediately, and I pushed my tongue inside, exploring every part of his mouth. Knowing that we needed to talk about what had happened the previous night, but right now, I needed to feel my mate inside me. "Make love to me. Claim me again, please," I whispered. Lamar complied by lifting me in his arms and taking me upstairs to our bedroom.

I didn't get time to say or do anything because my mate had ripped the clothes from my body before I knew it.

"Yes, that's how I like it," I groaned. The predatory look in Lamar's eyes nearly had me come, right then and there. Nothing could excite me more than Lamar losing control.

"Come here, my turn," I growled as I pulled Lamar close and ripped his close from his body. It was something that I had never done before, and Lamar looked surprised. Then, he groaned, something I couldn't decipher right before he attacked. God, it was so freaking hot. It was like the both of us had discovered a whole new side.

Lamar covered my mouth with his, using force, which, surprisingly, I liked very much. I grabbed his hair and pulled him slightly back because I wanted to look him in the eyes when I wrapped my fingers around his swollen shaft.

With my right hand, I held Lamar's hair in a firm grip so that he had to keep looking into my eyes. I let my left hand slowly slide south, straight toward his cock. Lamar closed his eyes and moaned when he felt my fingers around his sensitive erection, which was leaking precum steadily.

"Oh, dear God, yes yes," Lamar groaned as he started to move his hips in anticipation of my stroking. Lamar was well endowed, and I loved every inch of his massive cock. I grabbed my mate's shoulders and flipped him so he was beneath me. I had taken Lamar by surprise because I had never done that before. I was never powerful enough to flip my mate; now, apparently, I was.

Lamar lifted his upper body too; well, I didn't know what he wanted. Anyway, I placed both hands on his shoulders and held him down. "Stay down," I commanded. Lamar's eyes widened, but I could tell that he liked it, me commanding him. My mate obliged; I was gentle when I kissed his lips, then his jaw.

I started to lick and nibble Lamar's neck, where the skin was thin and thus very sensitive. He was shivering with need as he grabbed my hair. "Suck my dick," he growled. "Not yet. Patience, patience, my love," I growled back. Lamar grunted something I couldn't understand, but I didn't mind.

I slowly nibbled, sucked, and licked my way down Lamar's pecs before I let my tongue slide further. I playfully bit his nipple, making Lamar forcefully suck in his breath. "You like that, don't you, babe?" I whispered. Lamar didn't reply; he only grunted as he tried to push my head further down so I would suck his swollen cock.

I played with his nipples for a few minutes before I started to stroke his muscled abdomen. God, the man was beautiful, and all mine. Then, I finally reached Lamar's erection. I looked at my mate, opened my mouth, and closed my lips around the leaking shaft. I moaned when the first drops of precum exploded on my tongue.

"Yeah, baby, suck harder. I need more," Lamar moaned. Of course, I complied happily. I let my tongue swirl around the hard flesh, and then I dipped my tongue into the slit, which still was producing precum.

While sucking hard, I was a shifter; after all, I began to massage his balls. I loved to play with Lamar's testicles; they were huge and heavy. The moment Lamar pushed his hips up, I slid one finger inside his body. It was something that I had never done before. Lamar was an alpha male, and I wasn't sure if he would appreciate my finger in his ass.

It took him by surprise, but he pushed his hips up with even more force. "Oh God, baby. That feels so good. So damn good," Lamar softly moaned. I smiled because his reaction let me know that the man trusted me completely. An alpha would never allow someone to push his finger into his body. Well, unless it was his mate, or he had to trust that person. So not only was I Lamar's mate, but the man did trust me with his life, body, and soul.

"Now, let me," Lamar said, and before I could react, I was flipped so that I was underneath him. "Well, I'm all yours. So, have your wicked way with me," I chuckled. And Lamar did have his wicked way with me. First, he bit my neck; then he nibbled on my earlobe, which made me go wild. My earlobe was one of my erogenous zones that Lamar was well aware of.

Goosebumps broke out all over my body, and I was shivering violently with need, raw need. I wanted him, and I wanted him now, right this minute. "Fuck me, please. I need to be fucked right now, or I'll go crazy," I cried out.

Lamar didn't reply; instead, he inserted a second finger and then very quickly the third one. "Do it, now, for God's sake," I demanded. "Easy baby, I don't want to hurt you." "You won't, now fuck me, claim me," I urged, and Lamar complied.

My mate retrieved his fingers and positioned his shaft; then, he pushed in. He wasn't careful; Lamar pushed in hard until his cock was buried to the hilt. "Yes, that's it, that's it." I breathed. "I know what you want and what you need, baby," Lamar said as he pulled his cock nearly out of my body before pushing in again. In and out, in and out, it was heaven. I felt so full, so complete. Lamar grabbed my hips to steady me, and then he began to thrust in earnest.

My mate was quite forceful. If he hadn't grabbed my hips, then Lamar probably would have rammed me through the wall. Lamar pulled me up, and I positioned my legs left and right from his thighs. Then he lifted me and pulled me down again. I liked this position because this way, I felt every delicious inch of his hard length inside me.

"I'm close, so freaking close," I whispered out of breath. We went faster and faster, up and down, up and down, until I couldn't hold back any longer. Creamy, hot seamen jetted between our bodies. I knew that seeing my cock erupt would send Lamar over the edge, and I was right. "Oh, God," he said as he stiffened. Lamar grabbed my hair, and then I felt him filling me with his precious seed.

Chapter 04

"We still need to talk," I said as I sipped from my coffee. It was morning, and I had been so exhausted after our lovemaking that I had fallen asleep almost immediately. Lamar must have cleaned me afterward because there was no trace of seamen on my body when I woke one hour ago. I had opened the door to the garden for Milo. After breakfast I would take him for his walk.

"I know, baby." Lamar paused, then he said, "I thought about what you said. That you can hold your own and that you're not a weak person. That you need some kind of normalcy." Lamar paused. I looked expectantly at my mate and hoped and prayed that he saw the real me, and not a weak mate who needed protection, all day long.

"It won't be easy for me to let go, but I understand. I'll back off for now. However, if your life is in danger, then I will act accordingly," Lamar finally said. I smiled, and then I hugged and kissed the living daylights out of my mate. "Thank you, babe. I know that it wasn't an easy decision," I whispered. Lamar shook his head. "No, it wasn't," he softly replied.

"Anyway, I'm off now. I need to open the salon," I said. Lamar looked up. "Is Jason still sick?" he questioned. "Yes. I guess that it could take a week or so before he will be back at work," I replied. "Why does it take so long to recover from the flu?" Lamar asked, and I saw that the man really didn't understand.

"Yeah, well, humans don't recover that fast from the flu. I must add that Jason was pretty sick. So, I assume he won't be back until somewhere next week. I'm off now. I'll see you tonight, okay. If I sense danger, then I'll call you," I promised. Lamar didn't look happy, but he had to get used to the fact that I needed some kind of normal life again.

I stopped on my way out because I totally had forgotten to ask my mate about the case he was currently working on. "Babe?" "Yes?" "What case are you currently working on? You were gone for a long time yesterday."

I saw Lamar's face darken, which meant nothing good. "A young man was found murdered. It looked like strangulation, but we need to wait for to coroner's report," Lamar replied. "I can tell that there's more," I said. Lamar nodded. "The victim was in his mid-twenties, 5 ft 10, dark brown hair and brown eyes," he carefully explained

I felt the blood drain from my face. "It wasn't." "No, it wasn't Liam, but he could have been his twin," Lamar replied. "I don't understand. Are they after Liam and killed the wrong person by mistake? Does that mean that Liam is near Serigala Valley?"

My phone rang, and I saw that it was Jennifer. Shit, the salon. I took the call and told Jennifer that I was on my way. "I need to go, but we'll talk about this tonight, okay?" Lamar nodded, kissed me, and then I headed for the door.

When the salon came in sight, I saw three customers waiting. Thank God Jennifer was there, and she was talking and laughing with the two men and one woman. Christine, my other staff member would start her shift in two hours. "Mitchell, hello," Jennifer greeted, as she petted Milo.

Raoul Gutierrez would close the salon because Jennifer had worked all day, and Christine needed to get her young daughter from kindergarten. I had a dinner date with my handsome mate, and I would let nothing come between that. It had been a while that Lamar and I had dinner at a restaurant, so we both were looking forward to the evening. Plus, after the fight we had, we needed some quality time, just the two of us. Lamar had called me to let me know that he made reservations at The Red Dragon, my favorite Thai restaurant. I was pleasantly surprised because I love Thai food.

To my relief, Lamar hadn't been roaming around the salon, nor had one of the pack. So, he had gotten the message, and that I meant it. And I did mean it. I really needed a normal life again. Well, I was raised by humans, so it was the only life I knew. It was only normal that I clung to the life that I knew before everything in my life had changed. Besides, I was pretty proud that I still hadn't gone insane with all that had happened the previous months.

I drove up to the house I shared with my mate and frowned when I saw my father's car next to Lamar's vehicle. I parked next to my father's car and got out. I opened the back door, and Milo jumped out and immediately took off toward the front door.

My father and Lamar were in his study, where I joined them. First, I kissed my mate, and then I greeted my father. "Hey, dad. Not that I'm not pleased to see you, but what are you doing here?" I inquired. It was Thursday, and we would see my father on Saturday because Grandma

Natalya and Grandma Anichka had promised to cook Russian.

"I'm here because I have news about the whereabouts of Igor and Liam," my father said. That got my attention because I really wanted to talk to Liam and ask him why he had betrayed me. Something about a scheming Liam didn't add up. Something wasn't right; I felt it. And I knew that I wasn't wrong. So, yes, I was anxious to talk to my former friend.

The thought that someone was after Liam didn't sit well with me either. Why would they want to kill him? It just didn't make sense.

"Did you listen?" my father said. "What? I'm sorry, I must have spaced out for a few minutes," I apologized. "I said that Arkady is missing. He should be on his way home right now. But, he never boarded the plane," my grim-looking father said. "I don't understand. How is that possible? When was the last time he contacted you?" I inquired because this was bad.

"I'm going to Russia to look into the disappearance of Arkady." He eyed me and added. "And no, you can't come with me because it would be too dangerous." "That's bull, and you know it," I snapped. "This is exactly what I mean. You all see me as a weak shifter who is helpless. Well, guess what, I'm not. I can fight, and my tiger can, too. So we aren't helpless." I was upset that even my father was sheltering me from everything.

"I understand that you want to protect me; I really do, dad. But, please, understand where I'm coming from. My tiger is very powerful, and." "The answer is no, Mitchell," my father said, and he sounded adamant. I knew that further protest would be pointless.

"I need to go home now," my father said, stood, kissed my cheek, and then he headed for his car. I looked at my mate. Lamar shrugged as he to finished his coffee. "What just happened?" I said in disbelief. "Baby, you must understand why your father is so protective. For nearly twenty-six years, he thought that you were dead. Now, he has your back, and." "I know, I know. But still, it hurts that he thinks of me as weak," I whispered.

Lamar put his arm around my shoulder. "Alexei doesn't think of you as weak; believe me, he does not." I wasn't entirely convinced. "He told me that you are nearly as powerful as he is. That, in time, you will even be more powerful than he," Lamar said.

"Do you know when he's leaving for Russia?" "No, I guess somewhere in the morning hours," Lamar answered. Then I remembered that we had dinner reservations at The Red Dragon. "Since there's nothing I can do, right now, I'll take a quick shower, change my clothes, and then we will have dinner at The Red dragon," I said.

"Are you sure?" Lamar questioned. "Yep," I replied as I took the stairs that led to the bedroom with the adjacent bathroom. Lamar came into the bedroom; he put his hands on my shoulders and looked deep into my eyes. "Nor I, nor Alexei, think of you as weak. Sometimes you just need the help of family because the danger is too severe. Why don't you give Alexei a call before he flies to Russia? Let the man know that the both of you are okay," Lamar said before he kissed me on the top of my head.

I thought about that for a moment, and maybe, Lamar was right. "I'll call him now before we go to dinner," I promised. It wasn't that I was angry or anything. It just was, I don't know. Sometimes I felt so powerless, and other times it felt like I could take on the world.

"What's wrong with me? I snapped at my father for no reason. Yesterday I triggered a fight with you, again, for no reason," I whispered. "Sweetheart, there's nothing wrong with you. You went through quite a lot the previous months. You went from a normal human existence to being a tiger shifter. You had to learn about the preternatural world. You are constantly under attack, and until yesterday you were heavily guarded. No privacy, no going out with friends. Then, as the icing on the cake, it turned out that one of your best friends betrayed you. Well, I think that it's a miracle that you're still sane," Lamar said.

I sighed because what a mess. "Well, let's have a normal evening at The Red Dragon," I said smiling. Lamar nodded as he guided me to his car.

"This is nice," I smiled while I sipped from my red wine. "Yes, it is. We should do this more often. We need to go out more," Lamar replied as he drank his beer. The waitress came to our table again, and Lamar chose Chow Mein, and I ordered Kung Pao Chicken, which was my favorite.

I thought about the last time I've been here. I shook my head; it didn't do me any good to reminisce about that. "A penny for your thoughts," Lamar said as he was eyeing me intently. "Ah, it's nothing," I replied. "Baby? Talk to me. Don't shut me out," Lamar pleaded. I smiled ruefully, then I said, "I just thought of the last time I was here. I was with Liam, Justin, and Ralph," I explained. "Ah," Lamar returned.

"I want to go to my father's house before he leaves for Russia," I said. Lamar nodded as we continued dinner. We had a lovely evening; we chatted about the salon. And, how surprised I had been, not knowing that many of my customers were shifters. Lamar was right; we should do this more often.

We came out of the restaurant and walked to the car when I stopped Lamar. "Thank you. That was just what I needed," I said as I kissed my mate on his soft lips. "I enjoyed it very much. It was good to see you smiling and carefree again," my mate returned. Lamar then pulled me into his arms and kissed me. I felt all kinds of emotions coming from my mate as he kissed me. There was love, so much love, and adoration, but there was also fear. I wrapped my arms around his neck and kissed him back with everything I had.

Chapter 05

"I don't believe it," I said, and I knew that I sounded angry. "Calm down, baby. Alexei surely had a reason for leaving early," Lamar tried to soothe me. I gave him an indignant look. "He knew that we would come over to see him off," I said. "I know, baby. So, what do you want to do?" Lamar asked, looking expectantly at me.

"He knew that I wanted to accompany him to Russia and that, this time, I wouldn't take no for an answer. That's why he left before we arrived," I explained. I was so angry, so God damn angry.

"Baby? You really need to calm down. You don't want to lose control over your tiger," Lamar warned, and I saw him taking his phone. He was calling someone. "Who are you calling?" I growled. Yep, I was full of rage, and I felt my tiger emerge, which wasn't good. I knew that I needed to calm down because I had to control my tiger.

I looked up when I heard someone approach; it was Doctor Belinsky. "You called the doctor? Why?" I growled. "You're about to lose control, baby. I can feel the rage that's inside you," Lamar said in a calm, soothing tone, which made me even angrier. Lamar nodded at the doctor, and the next thing I knew, I felt a sting in my neck. After that, my vision became blurry, and then there was nothing.

When I opened my eyes, I saw a worried-looking Lamar, who was sitting beside me. I was in bed, in my old room. We were still at my father's estate. "What

happened?" I whispered; I felt confused, then it all came
back and struck me hard.

"Oh hell. Not again. What did I do this time?" I asked.
Me, losing control over my tiger one day and that it would
attack innocents was my biggest fear. "No, we were in time
to sedate you, baby. You didn't leave the house," Lamar
assured. I sighed in relief; I really needed to control my
tiger, permanently, not only on occasion.

"Well, I need to open the salon because Mason still is
stuck with the flu. Lamar had been surprised that Mason
was sick for days now and how that was possible. I
explained that it's different with humans; it can take a
while before they get well again when they get sick. I don't
know if Lamar understood.

Every time the phone rang, I hoped that it was my
father, letting me know that everything was alright. Even
though it was hectic, the day passed in slow motion. Mason
had called to let me know that he was getting better, and in
a few day's he would be back again. I had told him to take
it easy and wait until he really was healthy again.

I closed the door behind the last customer, and all I
wanted was to walk Milo and go home to my mate. My
father still hadn't called, which had me worried. A walk to
the park with Milo would do me good; being in the park
always relaxed me.

I leashed my dog, went outside, and closed the shop.
Milo was barking happily because he, too, loved the park.
"Come on, boy, let's go home," I said to my dog. It was
getting dark, which meant it wasn't safe for me to be out
on the streets again, let alone in the park.

I was about to open the car door when growling had me turn around. Milo growled, and before I knew it, several hyenas attacked me. Milo was fighting like a pro, and I was doing a good job defending myself. However, more and more of the damn beast appeared out of nowhere, it seemed. I knew that I would not win the battle this time and that I wouldn't be able to escape.

I managed to take down three hyenas before I felt a sting in my neck. Next, it was like hot lava was running through my veins. The last thing I heard was Milo barking like crazy.

I opened my eyes and closed them immediately because my head hurt so much. The next time I tried to open my eyes, I felt a bit better, but not by much. Now I noticed that my whole body hurt as well. I moaned in agony because the pain was excruciating.

I don't know how long I've been unconscious, but it felt like years had passed, shit! Still, I felt much better; the pain had lessened, thank God. Finally, I was slowly able to gather my thoughts and try to remember what had happened.

I looked around. I was in a room and guessed that the barred windows. Well, that wouldn't stop me from escaping. However, the moment I grabbed the bars, I was thrown back, hard. God damn. What the hell?

Then I heard muffled voices, but I couldn't decipher what they talked about. "No, please, you can't do that." Was that? No, surely not. Who else could it be? That was Liam's voice. I was sure of it. That would mean that he was back in Serigala Valley, which meant that Igor was probably back too. My father was in Russia to search for Arkady, great.

"Let's kill him, and no one has to find out what we did." This voice, I didn't recognize. "Oh, yeah? Well, what would Igor say if I told him that you murdered Mitchell, heir to the Balashov throne." That was Liam's voice again. It sounded like he was pleading for my life, which was odd.

Silence, then another voice spoke. "Liam is right. If we kill the little shit, then there would be hell to pay. We all know how deranged that son of a bitch is." "Igor is my mate, as you know, and that gives me the authority to speak in his name." That was Liam's voice, and he sounded much steadier.

They were silent again, and I strained to hear because maybe they were whispering. No such luck, damn. I noticed that the headache was gone, and my body almost felt normal again. What the hell had they injected? I really hoped that one of my grandmothers would be able to identify the sedative these idiots had used.

I had enough of people who poisoned me; I was getting angry. Maybe that was a good thing because maybe my tiger would be able to escape. Then again, if I lost control, no one could predict what would happen.

I thought about Liam, pleading not to kill me. I didn't understand because he had every reason to see me dead. Yet, here he was, telling, whoever they were, not to harm me. I looked out of the window; it was dark. How long was I here? Hours? Days? Months? My pulse sped up, which was a bad sign. I couldn't help it because the panic was slowly setting in. I concentrated on my breathing because I had to keep control over my tiger.

I was afraid that if my tiger got the upper hand, it would kill Liam for what the man had done to us. You must know that my tiger had been locked away for almost its entire existence, and that didn't make him a happy tiger. It knew that Igor and later Liam were to blame.

I looked outside again, hoping to see something familiar, something that let me know where I was held. As it was, I had no such luck. I walked over to the corner and sat down. There was no furniture, not even a chair to sit on, bastards.

I listened, but whoever had been arguing in front of my room, where gone, or so I guessed. I couldn't see much of the room because it was dark; all I noticed was that there was no furniture. It was even too dark to see what color the walls were. Were they brown, or yellow, or light blue even?

I felt my eyelids getting heavy, and as much as I tried to stay awake, I didn't succeed.

Chapter 06

I opened my eyes because something had woken me. At first, I was confused and didn't know where I was. Then I remembered I was kidnapped, but for the life of me, I didn't know why. I assumed that it had been Igor who had ordered the attack on me.

What I also remembered and what enraged me to a boiling point was Milo. What had they done to my dog? If they had harmed him, then there would be hell to pay. I was sure that Milo was still alive because I would have felt it otherwise. The bond with my dog was very strong.

What a fool I had been to refuse my mate's protection. Yep, I sometimes make stupid decisions. I only hoped that this one wouldn't cost me my life. I knew that I needed a miracle to get out of this room, alive.

The door opened, and I blinked because the lights in the hall were so bright, and I was still in this freaking dark room. My tiger reacted to the sudden change, and it wasn't happy. I took a few deep breaths and centered my mind, which I had learned from my two grandmothers. It helped, and it shouldn't have surprised me, but I did.

"Mitchell?" I knew that voice; it was Liam. "Liam?" I questioned. "Yes, it's me," he replied, and Liam sounded, well, afraid. "Why did you?" "Shut up, and listen. You need to get out of here because they are going to kill you. I could stop them by telling them Igor didn't want you harmed. It was a lie because he wants you dead," Liam explained.

I shook my head because I had to let it sink in. Apparently, the drug they used to kidnap me hadn't entirely left my body. I eyed him for a second or two. "You are aware that Igor will kill you if he finds out that you helped me escape?" I said.

"I know, but everything is better than to be Igor's bitch," Liam softly replied. "But, we have to go now because they can return any minute, and then they will kill us both," Liam whispered. I decided that I had no choice but to trust Liam; I rose and followed Liam.

It was now that I saw that I was in a house, and the room in which I was held was on the second floor. It smelled musty, which let me know that this house wasn't lived in. I wanted to ask where we were, but we needed to get out of there and fast.

We crept down the stairs and had almost reached the last step when Liam stopped abruptly. Voices were coming from what I assumed was the kitchen, and we had to pass the kitchen to get to the front door, damn.

After a few seconds, Liam moved again. We stood in the hall, and it appeared that Liam didn't know what to do. Liam motioned for me to start running because they would see us pass the kitchen one way or another. I looked at him, silently telling him that he should run as well.

I saw the fear in Liam's eyes and wasn't sure if he would follow me. Using my hands, I tried to let him know that we needed to start running simultaneously. Liam nodded, but he didn't look convinced. Then, suddenly, Liam pushed me and basically forced me to start running for the front door.

Liam had told me that the door would be unlocked, and I hoped and prayed that he hadn't lied. I stormed past the kitchen and to the front door; as expected, within seconds, the two thugs that had kidnapped me were in pursuit.

They were fast, but I was faster, and I ran without really knowing which direction I should go. All I wanted was to get away from my kidnappers as soon as possible. Suddenly I heard Liam scream, shit. I looked over my shoulder and saw that no one was running after me anymore.

That could mean only one thing, they had gone back, and now Liam was in danger. I stopped and turned, only to see the two men grab Liam and disappear inside the house. This was so not good. "Mitchell? Baby?" I turned and was about to release my tiger when I saw my mate. "I was trembling because my adrenaline had to be sky-high.

I was afraid to ask, but I needed to know. "Where's Milo? Do you know where my dog is?" I inquired. "Milo is home; he's safe. They had locked him up in your car. However, he broke free and ran back to our home. It was then that I knew that something terrible must have happened. Milo would never run away, so we immediately started searching for you.

"Breathe, baby, breathe," Lamar soothed as he held me tight. It was now that I saw Eric Stone, and Roy Addison, two of Lamar's betas. Scott Brown and Simon Dixon, the two best trackers of the McLaughlin Pack, were also there.

But there was no time for niceties; we needed to rescue Liam. "We need to get Liam. They're going to kill him," I urged. "What? Are you kidding me?" Lamar growled. I shook my head. "No, I mean it. He was the one who helped me escape. And because he helped me, they are going to kill him," I insisted.

Lamar sighed, and I knew that he would relent; he had to relent because I couldn't, in good conscience, leave him behind. "Are you sure that you want to save his life?" Lamar questioned. "Yes, I'm sure," I said. "Alright, then we need a plan to get him out of there," said Lamar. "Thank you," I said as I kissed him.

Even though Lamar would help rescue Liam, I knew he wasn't happy. That, however, wasn't of importance because right now, we had to get Liam. Lamar wanted to go home to make a plan to free Liam. I shook my head. "No, we need to get him out of there, right now. Liam is running out of time. Please, Lamar," I pleaded. "Alright, but only because I trust your instinct, baby. If you think he is worth saving, then I trust you," Lamar assured.

"We need as much information as we can get. What can you tell us about the layout of the house?" Eric Stone said. I told them what I knew, which wasn't much. Eric eyed Lamar. My mate shrugged, "Let's do it," he said. They discussed who would do what, and then we crept toward the house. I would stay close to Lamar because that he been his only demand. Well, I could live with that.

I saw Eric and Roy disappear to the right and Scott and Simon to the left side of the house. Lamar and I would enter the house through the front door. We had decided to take the risk and just storm inside, hoping to scare the living daylights out of them. As far as I knew, there were only two thugs inside.

It should be a piece of cake, but one never knew. We had to be careful because I had only seen two men, but there could be more in the house. Lamar and I would burst through the front door, and at the same moment, the others would enter the house through the windows.

We stood in front of the door and listened; maybe we could hear what they talked about. They could plan the death of Liam. "We need to kill him, you know that, right?" said a voice. "I don't know, man. He's Igor's mate, and no harm should come to him; he made that very clear." This was the voice of another person.

"He never has to find out that it was us who killed his precious mate. We could frame Mitchell," said the first voice. "Yeah, that sounds good. We could pull that off. Let's get him because the sooner I get out of here, the better. Igor can return any minute now, and I want to be gone before he arrives," said the second voice.

So, Igor was here, in Serigala Valley? Lamar looked at me, and I knew what he wanted to tell me. My mate kicked the door open, and we stormed inside. The two men stood in the hall, and I guess that they were on their way to the second floor. It was where they had held me, and now Liam.

We managed to take one man down, but the other managed to take the stairs and disappear. I shifted into my tiger and rushed up the stairs because I feared that he would kill Liam right then and there. I could not let that happen, no way!

Lamar was still fighting the man, who had changed into a freaking hyena; I should have known. I burst into the room where I knew I would find Liam. It turned out that I was right on time because the other one had changed into a hyena as well and was about to attack Liam.

As a human, Liam didn't stand a chance against a freaking hyena. "Step away from him; I'm asking you nicely," I growled. I had changed into my second form, so I stood on two legs, had arms with massive claws, and my face was almost tiger, but not entirely. It was a very odd sight, and I almost l had to laugh when I saw the shocked expression of the hyena.

I heard loud noises coming from downstairs; the betas and the trackers must have encountered others. So, there had been more than those two idiots in the house.

I turned to the hyena. "I'm not asking again," I growled. The hyena showed its teeth and then attacked Liam, who screamed in fear. "You idiot," I said right before I grabbed him and snapped his neck. Liam's eyes were huge, and his pupils too big, the man was in shock, shit.

I changed back and was pleasantly surprised that my mate handed me a sheet. My clothes hadn't survived the change, go figure. "He's in shock; we need to get him to Doctor Belinsky," I said. A moment later, Eric, Roy, Scott, and Simon joined us.

"Let me," Eric said as he gently lifted a motionless Liam into his arms. I looked at Lamar because was I missing something? Lamar shrugged but didn't say anything. Liam didn't protest when Eric lifted him in his arms and ascended the stairs. Lamar took his phone and dialed the doctor's number.

Chapter 07

Doctor Belinsky had Liam hooked up to an IV and had given him a mild sedative so he would sleep through the night. Eric had offered to stay with Liam, and Lamar had given his consent. Lamar was the alpha of the McLaughlin Pack, and it was up to him to approve or disapprove. Lamar had sent a cleaning crew over to the house to get rid of the dead hyenas.

"Thank you," I said when Lamar handed me a glass of red wine. "Are you going to tell me what that was between Eric and Liam? Why was Eric so, well, nurturing?" I questioned. We were alone; finally, everyone had gone home, except Eric, who was upstairs in the guestroom where Liam was resting.

I sipped from the wine while I looked expectantly at my mate. "I'm not sure, but the way Eric behaved, I would say that Liam is his mate," Lamar softly replied. "Say what?" I gasped because this was so not what I'd expected. "Are you kidding me? How can that be? I mean, Liam is Igor's mate, right?"

"We need to see if we can reach my father because he needs to know that Igor is back in Serigala Valley again. Lamar nodded, took his phone, and dialed. I frowned; why did it take so long for my father to answer the phone. "He isn't answering," Lamar said as he put the phone back on the table.

"That's not like him. He always answers his phone," I replied. "I know. That's what worries me. I don't like it."

"I don't like it either. Isn't there anything we can do?" I softly questioned. Despite everything and worrying about my father, I was beyond tired.

"I will do some investigation, see if I can trace Alexei's phone," Lamar offered. "Why don't you go upstairs and rest for a while. The kidnapping, the shifting, and Liam's rescue must have worn you out, baby," my mate added.

I nodded and was about to take the stairs to our bedroom when Lamar's phone rang. I stopped dead and stared at the phone. Lamar took the phone and checked the display. "It's Alexei," he said as he answered the phone. I was anxiously waiting for him to end the call and tell me if my father was alright.

Finally, Lamar put down the phone and eyed me. "Alexei is alright. He and Arkady are on their way home." "He found Arkady? Is he alright?" I asked because I needed to know that both men were doing okay. Lamar smiled. "Yes, both are fine. Arkady is just a bit bruised, nothing serious," my mate assured me.

"Bruised? He was attacked?" I growled because I didn't like what I just had heard. "Arkady is fine. You know that he can hold his own. The man is a fighting machine," Lamar assured me. "Now, go upstairs and rest for a few hours," Lamar urged. "Alexei and Arkady are boarding the plane as we speak. They have at least a fourteen-hour flight ahead of them," my mate explained. I conceded, but only because it was becoming difficult to keep my eyes open.

"Call me when Liam wakes? I want to talk to him," I said as I ascended the stairs. Lamar looked thoughtful; he said, "Why do you want to talk to him? The man poisoned you on purpose." I sighed. "I know, but something tells me that he isn't the bad guy. I can't explain it. I can only tell you how I feel," I told him.

"Alright, I will let you know the moment Liam wakes," Lamar promised. I nodded, then I turned and continued my way to the bedroom. I was tired, so tired.

"Baby? Wake up." I opened my eyes and saw Lamar sitting on the edge of the bed. "What's wrong," I sat bolt upright. "Nothing is wrong. You wanted me to wake you when Liam woke up. Well, he's awake," Lamar said.

"Why do you look so worried?" I questioned while I yawned and stretched. "Eric just confirmed what I already expected. He claimes that Liam is his mate," Lamar softly said. "Is Eric sure?" I asked because I was flabbergasted. "Eric said that he is one hundred percent sure," Lamar replied. "Oh, man. This could get very interesting," I said. "Yep," Lamar replied.

I got out of bed, dressed, and then knocked softly on the guestroom door where I knew that Liam was resting. Eric opened the door, but to my astonishment, he blocked the doorway. "Can I see Liam?" I softly asked. If Eric was indeed Liam's rightful mate, I had to respect his wishes. After all, I didn't want to start trouble for Eric. I knew that if Eric were rude, Lamar wouldn't be happy. That was so not an option.

"Why?" Eric didn't look happy; if anything, the man looked worried. I smiled reassuringly. "I want to talk to him. And I want you to know that I don't have any intention of harming Liam. I just need answers to the many questions I have," I said in a calm, soothing voice.

"I trust you, Mitchell. If you give me your word that you won't harm Liam," Eric said. I assured him that I wouldn't harm Liam, so Eric stepped aside so I could enter the room. I was shocked to see Liam, who was too pale, with hollow eyes and dark circles underneath. Liam looked haunted, and it broke my heart to see him like this.

"Are you here to hurt me?" Liam asked in a barely audible voice. I shook my head. "No, Liam, I'm not here to hurt you. I want to talk to you because I need answers only you can give me," I gently explained. I kept my voice soothing and calm so as not to spook Liam even more.

"Would you get me some water, please?" Liam asked Eric. The beta hesitated. "I will be alright. Now, go," Liam gently urged. Eric looked from Liam to me, but then he left. "Before you say anything, I need to apologize because it was never my intention to poison you," Liam looked expectantly up at me.

"I believe you," I said. Liam frowned. "You do?" he asked in a careful tone. I nodded. "Yes, I do. My gut feeling tells me that you are telling the truth," I said. "Why did you poison my moisturizer? Did you know that I was a tiger shifter? That those herbs would prevent me from shifting?" I gently questioned.

Liam opened his mouth to answer when the door opened, and Eric entered, two water bottles in hand. He looked at Liam. "Everything alright, here?" he asked. Liam nodded. "Yes, everything is fine," he replied, and Eric was rewarded with a small but genuine smile.

Liam told me how Igor had approached him and had changed into his tiger, right in front of Liam. The idiot didn't even have the decency to explain things to Liam. I can only imagine how afraid Liam must have been of Igor.

Igor threatened that Liam's youngest brother would be the first who would get to know his tiger. In other words, Igor's tiger would tear the kid apart. Liam had been scared to death, and that was why he had put the herbs into the moisturizer.

Then Igor had informed Liam that if I ever would find out about what he'd done, I would end his life. If not me, then Lamar, my mate. Liam had believed him then; the bastard had changed into a feral tiger. Liam had been paralyzed with fear when Igor, without warning, initiated the change.

Then the man had claimed that Liam was his mate. As expected, Liam had been in shock after he had seen Igor change into a very large tiger. But, unfortunately, he hadn't been able to get away from Igor. It seemed that the shifter was always close by. When Liam refused him, Igor started to terrorize him. Not only had Igor threatened to kill Liam's family, but to torture and kill his friends as well.

I had assured Liam that not all shifters were assholes and aggressive idiots. Liam hadn't looked convinced, though. I had told about Lamar and how gentle and nice my mate was. That Lamar adored me and that he would never hurt me.

"I know that Alexei and Lamar are nice because you gushed about them all the time. "Igor is Alexei's uncle, and we believe that he is responsible for taking my mother and me away from my father right after I was born. He let my father believe that we were dead," I whispered. I had trouble talking about that because we still hadn't found my mother.

Liam's eyes filled with tears, and I knew it was real; the man wasn't acting. "I'm so sorry for everything that I put you through. You must believe me, please?" Liam pleaded. I pressed my lips together. "I believe you, Liam," I said. Only now, we had to convince my mate of the fact that Liam was innocent. I didn't share that thought with Liam, though.

Chapter 08

"Baby, he poisoned you. Why are you defending him?" Lamar said. "I can't explain; all I'm asking is for you to trust me. Can you do that?" I urged. When Lamar didn't respond immediately, I added, "I won't treat him as the enemy, I can't, and I won't. When I was in his room, I felt the fear, literally felt it. The man is terrified of Igor."

Lamar considered me for quite some time. I waited patiently until the man was ready to give in. I knew Lamar would concede because he trusted my judgment, even though this was about Liam, who I once considered my best friend.

Lamar sighed deeply. "Alright, if that's what you want, but I also want to talk to him," my mate said. I frowned. "Liam is scared of you too. He thinks that you want revenge because he poisoned my moisturizer. Igor told him how protective a shifter can be when it's about his mate. He knows that you and I are mates," I explained.

Lamar frowned. "So, he thinks that all shifters are feral monsters?" my mate sounded baffled. I nodded. "Yep, I think that you hit the nail on the head, babe," I returned. "Jesus, I had no idea," Lamar whispered.

"Mitchell is right," said Eric as he stepped into the living room. We had heard Eric descending the stairs, so we didn't need to turn to know that he was on his way to see us. "How is he?" I asked, meaning Liam. Eric's smile was rueful; he said, "Liam is sleeping again." Then, Eric addressed me. "Is it normal that he sleeps so much? I mean." Eric raked his hand through his hair; he added, "I'm not familiar with humans. I never thought that my mate would be a human. So, I never was interested in how humans lived and. I don't know." The man sounded confused, and I could tell that he was worried sick. Well, this was about his mate, so who could blame the man?

"What are your plans with Liam," Eric asked, and I noticed that the man was tens. Lamar looked at me, and then he eyed Eric. "I was planning on treating him as a traitor who had poisoned my mate." I could see Eric tens up even more.

"However, Mitchell is convinced that Liam is a victim as well. And you know that I trust no one more than Mitchell," Lamar softly replied. "Thank you," said a soft voice from the threshold. I turned and smiled. "Liam, come in and have a seat," I motioned for Liam to sit down in the love seat so Eric could sit beside him.

Liam looked at me with so much uncertainty in his eyes that it nearly broke my heart all over again. "Are you hungry? I can fix you something to eat," I offered and laughed when his stomach chose that moment to growl. "I'll make you something to eat because you need to get your strength back," I said and left for the kitchen.

I made two chicken sandwiches because I knew that Liam loved those. And a huge glass of milk. "Chicken sandwich and milk," I smiled when I came back into the room again. I saw Liam's eyes lid up at hearing my words. It made me chuckle as I put the tray in front of him. I was satisfied to see him dig in. Eric looked at me and smiled as he nodded his thanks.

I cocked my head and smiled. "Dad is here," I whispered as I stood and headed to the hall to open the front door. "Thank God that the both of you are alright," I nearly yelled as I hugged my father tightly. Then, I hugged Arkady too, stunning the man.

To my astonishment, Milo came running, but he passed me and greeted Arkady. I was about to call my dog back when Arkady went to his knees and hugged Milo. My father eyed me, and then Milo and Arkady, then he shook his head. "Go inside; I will take Milo into the garden," said Arkady.

I had called my father and updated him about everything that had happened. At first, he, too, had been furious with Liam. However, after I explained about Igor, terrorizing poor Liam, he calmed down. He had promised me that he wouldn't retaliate against Liam. The man had been through a lot, so he didn't need another angry tiger shifter coming after him.

Liam paled when he saw my father enter the room. Eric tensed because he didn't entirely trust the situation. My father did the right thing, however. He first greeted Lamar because he was my mate. Then, he smiled as he crossed the room until he was in front of Liam and Eric. "How are you feeling, Liam?" my father asked, stunning both Eric and Liam.

Liam blinked a few times. "I'm tired and glad that Mitchell came back for me," he softly replied. Then, a loud bang that came from the kitchen made Liam jump and squeak in fear. "Sorry, I let something fall," Lamar yelled from the kitchen. My mate had offered to make coffee.

My father knelt in front of Liam. "Look at me, Liam," my father urged gently. When he had Liam's attention, he said, "We will protect you." "Why would you do that? I poisoned your son," Liam whispered. "True, but you helped my son escape. Mitchell didn't want to leave you behind. In fact, he insisted that Lamar and his betas would help him free you. That you were the victim, not the criminal." My father looked at me, and there was pride in his eyes; he added, "I trust my sons' judgment, which means that to us, you're innocent. That means that we will protect you," my father assured Liam again.

I saw that Liam blinked away the tears that were threatening to fall. Eric wrapped his arms around Liam and held him tightly. "Thank you, Alexei," Eric whispered. My father nodded, then he focused on me.

"Walk with me?" he said; I nodded as I eyed Lamar. "We'll be right back," I told him before I followed my father outside and into the garden. "Anyone else would have let Liam at the mercy of those two idiots. You wanted to save him. Why?" "I can't put my finger on it. But my gut feeling tells me that there's more to it than Liam betraying me. I'll bet that Igor will come for Liam. He wants him dead," I softly replied.

"I never believed that Liam was Igor's mate. However, he made that claim before Eric did. So, this could cause trouble if Igor insists that Liam is his rightful mate," my father explained. "Well, Igor won't get Liam because he's not his mate. "I tell you that if Igor gets the chance, he will kill Liam," I insisted. He wouldn't be able to kill his very own mate. Even though Igor is a cold-hearted bastard, he wouldn't be able to kill Liam. So no, Liam is not Igor's mate," I insisted.

My father nodded. "Change of topic. How is the investigation of those two murders going? You know the two young men who looked so much like Liam?" my father questioned. "Well, talk about a topic change," I chuckled. "And no, I don't know anything about that. Lamar didn't talk to me about that case." I paused, then I said, "Come to think of it, he should enlighten me. I mean, if it concerns Liam, then all of us should know what's going on."

Milo came running, followed by a smiling Arkady. It was strange to see Arkady doting on Milo. "It seems that he loves that dog of yours," my father remarked. "He does, doesn't he?" I returned. "Oh, before I forget. According to Liam, Igor is back in Serigala Valley. Somehow he's determined to get his hands on me," I said as I knelt to hug Milo.

"Not only is he back, but he's near. I can smell that bastard," Arkady growled. That got my attention and that of my father because he growled. My phone rang, it was Justin. "It's Justin, so I need to take the call. Let him know that Liam surfaced," I told my father.

"What are you going to tell him? Liam was missing for eight months; you need to come up with something plausible. Or my mother could cast a spell, making Justin forget that Liam had disappeared," my father offered, eyeing me intently.

I shook my head. "No, no spells. I'll come up with something, which means that I need to talk to Liam to corroborate our stories," I slowly replied. Liam had been gone for eight months. And I know that it sounds crazy, but I really hadn't given it much thought. Now, I had to make up a story, but one that Justin and Ralph wouldn't second guess.

"Hey, Justin," I greeted my friend. "Hi, Mitchell. Look, Ralph and I are going to La Petite Bistro for lunch. It would be great if you would join us," he said, and I could hear the uncertainty in his voice. Well, it had been a while since I had seen Justin and Ralph.

"That sounds good. I'll meet you there. What time?" I questioned, and the moment I said it, it felt right. Now that I thought back, I couldn't, for the life of me, remember the last time I had lunch or even dinner with my friends.

I told my father that I would have lunch with Justin and Ralph. He nodded his approval. "Let Liam know that you're having lunch with your friends," my father said. "I will watch Milo," Arkady offered as the dog walked over to him. It still amazed me that Milo was so fond of Arkady. While, in the beginning, he didn't even like the dog, or so it seemed.

Lamar wasn't so keen on me, having lunch with two of my best friends. Not because he didn't trust me. No, it was because he thought that it was too dangerous. Well, he wasn't entirely wrong. Things could get dangerous very fast if Igor really were back in Serigala Valley. I thought about Justin and Ralph; they were human. Would I bring danger to Justin and Ralph if we had lunch? I really couldn't tell because Igor already knew that Ralph and Justin were my friends. The bastard had never acted on that knowledge.

Chapter 09

"Are you sure that you up to it?" I asked my friend. "Yes, I'm sure. I missed going out with you, Ralph, and Justin," Liam replied. "Aright," I said. Then I softly added, "Are you okay with the story we're going to tell Ralph and Justin?" Liam nodded. "Yes, because everything is better than to tell them the truth," he said.

"Yep. We can't tell them that shifters really do exist," I replied. "Imagine," Liam chuckled. It was good to see him smile again. "Alright, let's go," I said. We took my car, and Lamar, Eric, and Dusty would follow us. I didn't object this time because it would be nice to have a backup if the shit hit the fan.

As we entered the restaurant, I saw that Justin and Ralph were already seated. I turned to Liam. "Are you ready," I gently questioned. "No, but let's do this," he softly replied. Well, to say that Ralph and Justin were shocked would be an understatement. "L. Liam?" Ralph stammered as he rose from the chair. Justin just stood there. It was apparent that he couldn't fathom that his friend was back after being absent for eight months.

"Yes, it's me," Liam softly replied, eyeing Ralph and Justin. It took a few seconds before it seemed to klick that it really was Liam who stood in front of them. Ralph and Justin hugged Liam tightly.

The waiter brought our drinks, Ralph and I had ordered a coke, Justin sparkling water, and Liam had ordered a sprite. Ralph and Justin were just staring at Liam, who began to feel uncomfortable. Well, we couldn't have that; this should be a celebration, not a staring in shock contest.

"I assume that you want to know where I was those previous eight months?" Liam began. Ralph and Justin nodded, eager to find out what had happened to their friend. "I'm really sorry, but it's something that I can't talk about right now. You need to trust that I will explain everything when the time is right. I could tell you a story, but then, I would lie, and that's not what I want," Liam had been sincere.

Before we headed out to La Petite Bistro, I had asked Liam what he wanted to tell Ralph and Justin. Liam knew that his friends would want an explanation for the eight months he had been gone. He also had told me that he didn't want to lie. So, Liam would say that he would explain everything when the time was right. I agreed wholeheartedly because nothing good could come from lying.

"So, you are living with Mitchell and Lamar now?" Justin questioned. Before Liam could answer, the waiter came and placed our order on the table. I had a chicken sandwich; Ralph wanted a vegetable soup with a bread roll. Liam and Justin both had ordered Roast Beef sandwiches. Liam looked at us, and then he said, "Yes, they were so kind to let me stay for as long as I want." Liam smiled at me, and I saw the gratitude in that smile.

Lamar and I had decided to let Liam stay in the guestroom with an adjacent bathroom. Plus, that particular guestroom was very spacious. So, he could retreat and have his privacy if he needed it.

Then an idea came to mind; only, I didn't know if Lamar would be so happy with my plan. I suggested that Ralph and Justin would spend the night at my place. We had a lot to talk about, and it would distract Liam. The man was absolutely terrified of Igor.

So, I told them about my idea that Ralph and Justin would spend the night at my place too. They were, of course, game. By the way Liam's eyes lid up, I knew that I had said the right thing. Now, all I had to do was inform my mate of my plans. I walked outside of the restaurant to talk to Lamar. As expected, he wasn't thrilled at the idea of Ralph and Justin spending the night at our home. It was not because he didn't like them, but he didn't want to put them in harm's way.

If Igor decided to attack, my friends would be in grave danger. I told Lamar that we had enough backup from the tigers and the wolves to protect us. Plus, it would do Liam a world of good. After talking and explaining everything to my mate, Lamar finally conceded, as I knew he would.

After lunch, we first went to Ralph's apartment and then to Justin's place. We drove in my car to the house. I didn't want too many cars in front of the house because if Igor were near, he would notice. Liam didn't have his car anymore; Igor had made sure of that. The bastard had sold Liam's car without so much as even letting the man know.

Even if Liam had known, he hadn't been able to stop Igor. Liam still was terrified of the bastard. I parked the car in front of the house and was pleasantly surprised when Lamar had placed additional beds in Liam's room. I had told my mate that, I too, would spend the night with my friends. My mate had chuckled and said that he didn't expect anything else. Yep, my mate was the best.

We spent the afternoon in the garden with Milo and Arkady. The man not only adored my dog, but he had gotten very protective of me. I don't know what happened while he was in Russia, but somehow his attitude towards me had changed.

The sun was shining, and we had fun playing with Milo, and Lamar provided us with soft drinks and snacks. My father had provided ten more soldiers, just in case Igor would decide to attack. We knew that the bastard would try and take Liam. Liam had admitted that he was terrified that Igor would get to him. I had told Liam that my family would not let that happen. I also had explained that I wasn't a regular shifter, but one with a second form, which is even more deadly.

I knew that my tiger would tear Igor apart if he took one step onto the premises. Unlike my father, we had no fencing around our property. Lamar and I had decided that we didn't want nor need it.

We had, however, tight security, like cameras, surrounding the premises. We wanted to install motion sensors. However, that wouldn't be wise because the animals who lived near the house would set the alarm off repeatedly.

We would need an expert to install the correct motion sensors, which wouldn't react to small animals. It wasn't really my thing, so I don't know much about it. All I knew was that we still didn't have motion sensors. So, I was grateful that my father had sent us ten of his best soldiers.

Even though I didn't see Lamar, I knew that my mate was near; I felt his presence. My mate had been adamant about that; he would stay out of sight but still close by and ready to intervene should Igor decide to attack. I also knew that we were heavily guarded and that those soldiers were everywhere. My friends, who all were human, wouldn't notice their presence.

Lamar had promised to cook dinner for us, and I had asked if he wanted to cook lasagna. I just love lasagna. "Does it matter where we sit?" Justin asked. I shook my head. "No, sit anywhere you want," I told my friends.

Dinner was loud because everyone was talking to everyone. We had invited my father and Arkady to join us for dinner. "This really is good," Ralph complimented my mate. Well, I must say that Ralph likes almost everything. But, the lasagna was heaven, just the right amount of spices and sauce. Many people think that cooking lasagna is easy. Well, it's not that easy, especially if you start from scratch, which is what my mate had done.

Eric sat beside Liam, and they were quietly talking. Arkady eyed me intently, and my father had a conversation with Ralph and Justin. I sat, ate, and watched everyone interact with each other. For a moment, just a short moment, it all felt, well, normal

After we finished the meal, Lamar and Eric served dessert, cheesecake with fresh strawberries, and of course, whipped cream. "Oh man, can I come and live here too?" Ralph begged, which made me laugh. "Oh no, buddy. Tomorrow you're off to your apartment," I laughed; Ralph scowled, which made me even laugh harder.

"We will invite you to dinner, on occasion," I promised him and Justin. Eric sat close to Liam, and it looked like Liam was slowly getting his old self again. I had asked him if he did mind that Eric was with him all the time. Liam had blushed when he admitted that he liked Eric a lot. I knew that it must be the mating pull that he felt.

Before moving Liam into our home, I talked with the man for hours. He had told me that Igor once said that if he couldn't have Liam, no one would. I knew what that meant, and so did Liam. The man was terrified and a bit naive, but he wasn't born yesterday.

Lamar had told me that if Liam wouldn't feel comfortable around Eric, then he would send the shifter home. So, I knew that Lamar would be pleased to hear that Liam liked Eric very much.

It was near midnight when we went to our bedrooms. I would spend the night with my friends in the guestroom. "Come here, and let me kiss you goodnight," Lamar growled as he grabbed me and slammed our mouths together.

Chapter 10

What the hell? I woke to a yelling and screaming Liam. The light was already on, and a wild-eyed Ralph and Justin watched in horror at Liam. The man sat upright and looked terrified, and he wasn't awake. Liam was having a nightmare, and it must be a horrifying one. He babbled about how Igor had forced himself on him and how the tiger shifter beat him.

My tiger was full of rage because it felt the fear that rolled off Liam in waves. Plus, my tiger seemed to understand every word Liam spoke, which enraged it even more. Ralph looked at me, his eyes wide with fear. "What is he talking about," he whispered while he slowly moved closer to Justin.

I sighed because what could I say? Liam had spilled the beans about the preternatural world to other humans. Usually, it would mean severe punishment. However, in this case, Liam had spilled it while having a nightmare, so he wasn't to blame. If anything, this would go on Igor's account because he was the cause. Well, he would pay for everything he had done to Liam, my family, and me.

Liam suddenly screamed, and it was so unexpected that it had me startled. Then, the door burst open, and Lamar and Eric stormed inside. Still, Liam didn't wake, which was weird. Eric was at Liam's side in seconds. The wolf shifter carefully took Liam in his arms and started rocking him gently.

"What the hell is going on?" Lamar whispered. I told him that Liam had a vivid nightmare and that he had spilled the beans about the preternatural world. Lamar frowned but didn't reply. Meanwhile, Ralph and Justin looked from me to Lamar. Then, they watched Eric, who had a slowly awakening Liam in his arms.

Liam woke in confusion, which was expected after the nightmare he had suffered. Eric was whispering words of love and devotion in Liam's ear. It seemed to work because Liam calmed down. I eyed Lamar in question because I didn't know what to do or say. Lamar was the alpha of his pack, so it was up to him to handle the situation.

"I would like everyone in the living room. Could you handle Ralph and Justin?" To hear the voice of my mate inside my head had me startled for a moment. I nodded. "Ralph, Justin, would you come with me into the living room, please?" I asked in a soothing tone. Ralph eyed Justin, and it seemed that both men didn't know how to react. Well, granted, it wasn't an everyday situation.

"No harm will come to you, I promise," I said as I kept my distance. "You know me. I'm still the same Mitchell," I assured when they didn't move. "Are you?" Ralph finally replied. I smiled. "Yes, I am." "What was Liam babbling about? What are shifters?" Justin quietly questioned.

"That's what we want to explain to you, but not here. We need to give Liam some time with Eric," I explained. Ralph observed Eric and Liam. Justin looked weary. "Is he safe?" Ralph whispered. I knew that he meant Liam. "Absolutely. There's no safer place to be for Liam because Eric will protect him with his life," I gently insisted.

"I, for one, would like to know all about, well, what Liam was babbling about," Justin softly said. "Then come with us," I said. And to my astonishment and joy, Justin moved toward me and motioned for Ralph to do the same. Ralph was reluctant, but then he, too, moved toward me.

"Come with me, and I will make us some coffee," I said. "Or something stronger," Justin said. "Or something stronger," I echoed, smiling. I really hoped that I could convince my friends that, yes, we carried an animal inside, and no, we wouldn't harm them.

Ralph and Justin both accepted a tumbler with whiskey. I drank coffee, as did Lamar. "So, are you going to tell us what Liam was talking about while having the scariest nightmare of his life?" Justin questioned. He sounded curious and a bit angry; I guessed it was on Liam's behalf. That was good because it meant that he wasn't that scared anymore.

I eyed my mate, and when Lamar nodded, I began to explain. "Before I explain things, I need you to know that we would never harm you. If anything, we will defend you, like we defend Liam. Like we defend all of our friends and family," I softly said.

"I believe you, and I trust you," Justin finally said after eyeing me for what seemed like hours. "Thank you," I replied. Ralph looked at Justin. "What? You know as well as I do that Mitchell has never given us reason not to trust him," Justin said. Then he looked at me and added, "I still consider you as one of my best friends. If that means that your tiger is my friend too, then that would be even better."

Liam had talked a lot in his sleep, and Justin and Ralph weren't idiots. I hadn't denied anything Liam had babbled.

"So, you really can change into a white tiger?" Ralph softly questioned. I nodded. "Yes, I can." "Why did you lie to us all that time? Didn't you trust us enough to share your secret?" Ralph sounded more; well, angry wasn't the right word. No, he sounded lost.

"Let me explain things to you, and for that, I need to start from the beginning, so you understand," I began. Ralph and Justin both nodded. I noticed that they seemed more at ease, but that could be because of the whiskey. So, I started to explain everything, from start to finish, so to speak.

Eric and Liam had joined us after Liam had calmed down enough. I stared out of the window. The night had disappeared to make room for the day. A long silence followed after I finished explaining. I really hoped that we could stay friends.

"As I said earlier, I still consider you as one of my best friends. Nothing has changed," Justin said. "Me too," Ralph assured me. Then all eyes were on Liam. "How are you holding up?" Ralph softly asked. "Alright, I guess," Liam replied as he leaned even closer to Eric. "Good. I know that I'm not as strong as you guys, but I will kick this Igor person's ass if he comes near Liam," Ralph said, and the man sounded very determined. "What he said," Justin pointed at Ralph.

Lamar smiled, and I saw a satisfying look on Eric's face. I smiled too because I knew that Ralph and Justin wouldn't stand a chance against Igor. They knew that too, but even so, they were ready to defend their friend, which made them golden in my book.

The doorbell rang, and I went to let my father into the house. He had gone home last night after I had assured him that we were safe. I had promised that we would call the minute Igor showed up. I knew that Igor was a very strong shifter. I also knew that I was getting more powerful with each day that passed. My father had told me that, one day, I would be the strongest tiger shifter ever.

Since I wasn't the strongest shifter ever, yet, I had to consider that Igor would be able to take me down. He was a force to be reckoned with. My father had warned me more than once about how devious Igor was in a fight.

My father had been stunned when I had told him that even though I didn't know how to fight shifters, my tiger apparently did. After all, my tiger had proven that more than once that he was perfectly able to defend himself. My father believed me because he knew that I didn't lie.

Ralph eyed me; he said, "I know that you wouldn't harm any of us. But, would you mind not changing into your tiger for now? Well, at least not when I'm near." Ralph looked so guilty. "No problem. You will let me know if you're ready to meet my tiger," I assured my friend. Ralph nodded, and I was rewarded with a small smile.

Ralph still didn't feel at ease in my company or the other shifters, and I really couldn't blame the man. But, Justin was another story because he was anxious to meet my tiger. So, I had to promise him that soon, I would shift and that he would meet my tiger.

Chapter 11

"He's near. I can feel it," a trembling Liam whispered. Lamar immediately reacted. He grabbed the phone and started dialing. Even though Liam wasn't Igor's mate, he still seemed to, somehow, have a connection with the shifter. Lamar was curious about that connection. He hoped that maybe, it could help them locate and capture Igor. As it was, Liam still was terrified of Igor. So, Lamar would have to wait until Liam was ready to put the link they apparently shared into use. Lamar had called my father, who was on his way right now. Of course, he would bring Arkady and some well-trained soldiers. Also, Scott Brown and Simon Dixon were on their way and would arrive shortly. They were Lamar's best trackers.

Justin and Ralph looked frightened, which I understood because they saw Liam trembling with fear. Eric wrapped his arms protectively around Liam and held him tightly. "We won't let Igor near. The way I know him, he is taunting us. He might be on the premises, but Igor won't come near the house. Not yet, anyway," my father said from the doorway.

"Hey," as I hugged my father. "Hey, son. How are things here?" my father inquired as he eyed Liam and Eric. "We are on high alert, as you can imagine," I answered. My father nodded as he took the offered coffee from Lamar.

An angry-looking Arkady stood in the doorway, eyeing everyone. I could tell that he couldn't wait to put his hands around Igor's neck and choke the life out of the shifter. Well, that would have to wait because we first had to capture the bastard.

Scott and Simon arrived sometime later and informed us that it was indeed Igor that had been near. However, the shifter didn't seem to have entered the premises. "The scent was faint, but it was there. So, we don't think that he breached the security but stayed outside the gate," Simon informed.

"I knew it. I knew that it was him," Liam whispered. "Hush, baby. No one will come near you. Everyone here will protect you," Eric soothed. It took several hours before my father and Lamar were absolutely sure that Igor had left. Liam slowly relaxed, as did Ralph and Justin. They had been equally afraid as Liam. Still, they had said that they would help defend Liam against Igor should it become necessary.

My father's phone rang, and after one look at the display, he excused himself to take the call. This was odd because he had never done that before. "Later," he said at my questioning look. I didn't reply because I knew that I simply had to wait.

It was after ten in the evening when Lamar, my father, and I were finally alone. Justin and Ralph were in their guestrooms, and Liam and Eric also had retreated to their room. I eyed my father. "So, who called you this afternoon?" I questioned. He sighed. "That was your Uncle Dimitri," he said.

I opened my mouth and then closed it again because I didn't know what to say. I thought that I knew all my uncles from my father's side. Apparently, I was wrong. I glanced at Lamar, and he looked just as surprised as I felt.

"Dimitri is two years older than me, and he lives in Russia," my father explained. Well, that was not good enough. "Why didn't you tell me about him? I mean, he's family, right?" I said. "He is family, but I haven't spoken to him in." he paused, then added, "about twenty-five years."

"Why not? Did you have a fight?" I asked because now I was intrigued. I had another uncle who I had never met. Hell, my father had never mentioned him before. "Why did he call?" I questioned; this was like pulling teeth. I had to drag every word out of the man.

"Dimitri is on his way to Serigala Valley as we speak. He wants to talk to me. That's all I know," my father said. "I want to meet him," I said. My father smiled. "Of course you do," he chuckled. "So, you're not close to Dimitri? Because your other brothers did move to Serigala Valley, only he, Dimitri, did not. I wonder why?" I said.

My father shrugged. "I don't know. But what I do know is that he spent a lot of time with Igor. So, that could be the reason he stayed in Russia. I really wouldn't know," my father sounded sincere, and I believed him.

"I wonder what it is that he wants. He must have a reason for coming here," I said. "Well, we have to wait until the man arrives," Lamar chimed in. I nodded because my mate was right, but still, I didn't like it. My Uncle Dimitri was on his way to Serigala Valley; why? What was it that he wanted? "You look skeptical," my father said. "That's because I am," I returned. "When can we expect him to arrive?"

"Can I speak to you in private?" Dimitri addressed my father in Russian; he hadn't spared me a glance. I couldn't care less, but I did care about my father, and if Dimitri would pose a danger, then I would do something about him. I stunned Dimitri when I said, in Russian, "My father and I don't have secrets from each other. Not if it concerns family."

Dimitri arrived at my father's estate, and it was where Lamar and I were too. The man didn't want to go to my place. Well, that was fine with me because I didn't want him there anyway. Eric, Liam, Ralph, and Justin were still at my house, as were Roy, Scott, and Simon for protection. Simon and Scott were trackers, but they could hold their own in a fight.

Dimitri eyed me intently; I stared back at him. Then, he suddenly said, "Where did you learn the Russian language?" It took me a second to notice that Dimitri was addressing me. "I didn't learn; I just know," I answered. "I don't believe you," Dimitri replied. "Well, I don't care what you think, Uncle Dimitri," I drawled.

My father shot me a warning look. Then, to Dimitri, he said, "My son doesn't lie, so don't ever speak to him like that again." Dimitri looked at my father in disbelief. "Don't," my father said in a barely audible voice. Dimitri, who had opened his mouth to retaliate probably, closed it again.

"Mitchell is the real deal, so you better start respecting him," said a female voice from behind me. It was Grandma Natalya Balashov. She had spoken softly, but the command in her tone didn't go unnoticed. "Mother? How are you?" Dimitri said as he crossed the room and hugged her tightly. I felt my grandfather before I saw him enter the room.

The man just stood there, watching his mate and their son hug each other. "Father, how good to see you," Dimitri smiled, and it was a genuine one. The man really loved his parents, I felt it.

So, did that mean that Dimitri really thought I was a fraught? That I was after the Balashov fortune? Grandpa Nicolay held Dimitri at arm's length, looked him in the eyes, and said, "Son, I know that you want to protect the family, but Mitchell really is Alexei's son and our grandson." "How can you be so sure?" Dimitri countered. The man still didn't believe that I really was Mitchell Balashov.

Arkady, who had walked Milo, came into the room, Milo still on the leash, which made me frown. Then, before I could ask why my dog was still leashed, Arkady said, as he gazed at Dimitri, "Milo is restless." I understood; it meant that Milo didn't like it that Dimitri was in the house. My dog had changed, and even though he still loved to cuddle, he had become extremely protective.

I unleashed Milo and commanded the dog to stay at my side, which he did because Milo was well trained. Arkady smiled and shook his head. Dimitri stared from Arkady at me and then back at Arkady again.

Arkady didn't say anything but motioned for Dimitri to follow him, which, to my astonishment, the man did. I eyed my father in question because what had I missed? "Dimitri and Arkady are very close," my father explained.

“Aren’t you worried that Dimitri will try and convince Arkady that I’m a fraud?” I asked.

My father shook his head; he said, “No, Arkady is loyal to me; of that, I have no doubt. If anything, he will tell Dimitri that you really are my son.” He paused, then he said, “Remember that at first, Arkady didn’t like you one bit?” I nodded because, yes, I remembered well. I had told my father that I was convinced that Arkady hated my guts. Now, the man knew that I was the real deal, and he had started to like me. So, yes, maybe my father was right, and would Arkady tell Dimitri that I really was Mitchell Balashov, Alexei and Nadia’s son.

Chapter 12

I sat at the kitchen table, drinking my coffee while waiting expectantly for my Uncle Dimitri to arrive. Obviously, my father didn't want him staying at the house while the man was hostile toward me. Arkady had left to get Dimitri, who was staying at the hotel. I was curious about what the man had to say. And for the real reason why he had come to Serigala Valley.

Finally, after what seemed like forever, the front door opened, and in walked Arkady, followed by a serious-looking Dimitri. They sat down, and my father politely offered them coffee.

Dimitri eyed me intently, then he softly said, "I need to apologize for my rude behavior." To say that I was baffled was an understatement. I stared at him, not really knowing what to say. Dimitri went on. "It's true that I didn't believe it when Alexei claimed to have found you. His son, of which we were convinced had died during birth." The man paused again, looking strangely at me.

"It was stupid of me to believe everything Igor said about you," Dimitri admitted. I nodded. "Yeah, maybe it was, but Igor is your uncle, and that's why you trusted him, right?" I said. "Yes, that would be correct. Still, I shouldn't have assumed; I should have talked to Alexei as well. A story always has two sides. And I'm ashamed to admit that I only listened to Igor. And I'm sorry that I believed him on his word. I hope that you can forgive me," Dimitri softly replied.

"There's nothing to forgive. You trusted your uncle. Igor is family and therefore should be trustworthy. But, unfortunately, he's not. In fact, he forced Liam, one of my best friends, to poison me with herbs to prevent me from shifting. Then, when we found out, Igor kidnapped Liam and falsely claimed that he was his mate. As a result, Liam is here, and he is traumatized by what Igor did to him." I paused because I was getting emotional.

"Are you okay, baby?" Lamar inquired. I nodded, then I continued. "Plus, he's the one responsible for my mother and my disappearance. He deprived me of growing up with my parents, of experiencing growing up in a loving home as a shifter. We know that my mother isn't dead because we lifted her coffin; it was empty," I said bitterly.

Dimitri sighed deeply. "I want to talk about the lies Igor told me if that's alright," he said. "Sure," I said because I wanted to know what that conniving SOB had said, trying to poison Dimitri's mind.

"For one, Igor told me that Alexei had put a price on his head, one million dollars." I gasped because this was more than ridiculous. Dimitri continued, "He claimed that Alexei kidnapped Liam, his true mate. He convinced me that you," Dimitri pointed at me. "Are an imposter who is after the Balashov fortune."

"This is more than ridiculous. The man is insane," I said. "Yes, he is. And I know that now. You must understand, I live in Russia, and because of Igor, I didn't have contact with my family here, in Serigala Valley. That gave Igor the time that he needed to poison my mind," Dimitri explained. In which he succeeded, but that was a thought I kept to myself.

I eyed my Uncle Dimitri, and the expression in his eyes said what I needed to know. "There's more, isn't there," I questioned. He nodded. "Yes, there is. And you are very perceptive," Dimitri chuckled. I smiled; it was good to see the man relax. Now that he explained why he was so suspicious of me, it did make sense. It seemed that Arkady had a really good conversation with Dimitri the previous night.

"Anyway," Dimitri began addressing me. "Igor claims that he didn't have anything to do with the, well, death of Nadia. In fact, he insisted that she was dead and was buried in Serigala Valley, as are you, Mitchell. I now know that this was a lie as well," Dimitri sounded bitter, and rightly so. His uncle, whom he had trusted, turned out to be a lying psychopath who was hell bend on killing Mitchell. Why? That was anyone's guess.

"I'm convinced that my mother is alive, and we will find her," I insisted. "We will, son. We will find her," my father said. Dimitri pressed his lips together; he softly said, "If you let me, then I would like to join my family again." I had to think about that one, and my father too because he didn't react immediately.

I said, "What about Igor?" Dimitri frowned. "What about him?" he questioned, looking confused. "You were loyal to Igor for many years," I explained. "The man has lied to me for many years. He played me for a fool, and I'm not a fool. So, I'm done with him," Dimitri said.

Since this wasn't my call, I looked at my father, whose face was unreadable. My father looked at me and then at Arkady. I nodded, and so did Arkady. "If you're prepared to pledge your loyalty to my streak, then you are welcome to join the family," my father said.

Dimitri didn't hesitate to tell us that he would like nothing more than to be part of the family again. So, he wanted to pledge his loyalty immediately, and my father agreed. It also meant that Dimitri would move into the house because it was safer. Dimitri had to watch out for Igor now that he was done with the shifter. Igor wouldn't take it kindly that Dimitri was now loyal to my father, and the shifter was a force to be reckoned with.

My father eyed me; he said, "Are you still safe in your home?" I nodded because, yes, I still felt that I was safe in the home I shared with Lamar, my mate. "If it gets too dangerous, then I'll let you know," I promised. We had lunch, and after that, Arkady drove Dimitri to his hotel to get his belongings and move into my father's estate.

******

"Perfect, as always," Mrs. Alston smiled as she took her credit card and put it in her purse. I guided her to the door. I had decided to go to work because the salon needed my attention. Jason, my manager, was good at his job, but it was my business, so The Cutting Edge Hair Salon needed my attention.

I looked up when the doorbell jingled, letting me know someone was entering the salon. The hairs at the back of my neck stood on end when I smelled hyenas. Shit, what was I supposed to do? There were customers and staff present at the salon.

And was that fear I smelled? Yes, it was. I reached for my cell phone, and I didn't know what stopped me from calling Lamar or my father. The two hyenas didn't look menacing. Hell, they didn't even pretend to intimidate me.

What the hell? I needed to act as normal as possible because humans were in the salon.

Two wolf shifters who were waiting for their turn rose and started growling. One look from me, and they sat down again. It wouldn't do me any good to have two shifters start a fight with the two hyenas. Not in front of humans, anyway.

They slowly came closer. "We don't want trouble, but we need help," the one with the brown hair softly said. "Sanctuary," the other one, who had light brown hair corrected. That got my attention. "Take a seat at the table," I told the two hyenas. They didn't move but kept staring at Billy and Adam, two shifters from my pack. Yeah, I belonged to the McLaughlin Pack because I was mated to their alpha. And I belonged to the Balashov Streak because their leader, Alexei Balashov, was my father.

I eyed Billy and Adam; then my focus was on the two hyenas again. Billy and Adam won't harm you," I told them. "As the alpha mate of the McLaughlin Pack, you have my word," I said and kept my tone gentle. These two hyenas didn't pose a threat; if anything, they were afraid. I wondered what had them so spooked.

"You know what, follow me," I urged because I needed them away from my customers, and I needed to call my mate and my father. Billy and Adam looked uncomfortable, and I knew why. They didn't want me alone with two hyenas, which I understood. "I'll call Lamar to let him know what's going on," I said. "We really don't want to leave you alone with them," Adam softly said. Even though Billy and Adam were still so young, they were very protective. "Alright, follow me, but, the both of you need to stay calm, no aggression," I said. Both young men nodded, I was the alpha mate, and they obeyed me as they did Lamar.

When I stepped into my office, I directed Adam and Billy to one side and the two hyenas to the other side of the room. "I need to call my mate who is the leader of the McLaughlin Pack, and my father, leader of the Balashov Streak," I said, addressing the two hyenas. "I gave you my word that no harm will come to you," I assured. Then I took my cell phone and started dialing.

Chapter 13

The door opened, and Lamar, my father, Arkady, and Dimitri stepped into my office. My office wasn't that big, and with so many people, the room became very crowded. However, I knew that nor Lamar nor my father would take the two hyenas anywhere before talking to them.

"We seek sanctuary," the one who introduced himself as Arden Spencer softly said. I noticed that they didn't make eye contact. It was a sign that they were very submissive, and I wasn't sure if I liked that. To me, it was evident that they had suffered, probably at the hands of their leader. I would ask them about that later.

The two hyenas were Arden Spencer, twenty years, and Felix Mills, also twenty years. They were fed up with all the aggression of their leader. It turned out that the leader of the hyenas was a tyrant of the worst kind. Arden and Felix were tired of fighting and hurting innocent people and shifters alike. Titus Karr, leader of the hyenas, was known for his sadism; he loved to torture clan members. Lamar knew Titus, and he didn't like the shifter. Then there was Travis Karr, Titus' brother; he seemed even worse than Titus.

"Will you grant us sanctuary? If not, then we need to know because if we can't stay, then we need to get away from Serigala Valley as soon as possible," Arden said. It looked like Dimitri wanted to say something; he opened his mouth and closed it again. The man had a strange look in his eyes. "By now, Titus will know that we ran away. If he catches us, we won't survive," said Felix. Dimitri growled, my father and Lamar frowned.

"He will torture us until we stop breathing." Arden eyed me; he added, "Do you have any idea how long it takes to torture a shifter until he dies? Well, I do." Then Arden turned his head, but not before I had seen the unshed tears.

Even though I was convinced that Arden and Felix had spoken the truth, my father wasn't. Of course, I wanted to grant them sanctuary, but it wasn't my call to make; it was up to Lamar or my father. *"I want to grant them sanctuary,"* I used the mind link I shared with my mate. *"I'm not sure, baby. I don't know them, and hyenas are treacherous creatures,"* Lamar replied through our mind link.

I told Lamar that I was sure that Arden and Felix had spoken the truth. He asked me if I was sure that the two wouldn't pose a threat. I said that no, they wouldn't, that I didn't sense any kind of dishonesty. These two hyenas wouldn't betray us, of that I was sure. Lamar, however, wasn't convinced.

Dimitri motioned for my father to follow him out of my office. I looked at Lamar, who shrugged.

"We need to go," Arden said all of a sudden. Felix looked at me, and I could tell he didn't want to leave. Didn't they have family or partners?

"Do you have family members who are still living at the clan?" I questioned. I don't know why, but something inside me let me know not to let Arden and Felix run away.

By now, Titus must be searching for them. These two weren't a match for a leader who was on the warpath.

The door opened, and my father entered the room, followed by Dimitri. "You can stay at my house. As the leader of the Balashov Streak, I will grant you sanctuary. First, however, you need to pledge your loyalty," my father said.

My father granting Arden and Felix sanctuary confused me because why would he do such a thing? And what was it with Dimitri? Why did he need to speak to my father in private? Arden and Felix looked at me as if they were asking permission.

My father would take Arden and Felix to the estate. Lamar would go with them as well. Billy and Adam resumed their seats in the salon until it was their turn to get a haircut. Arkady and Dimitri followed my father out of the salon, and I was alone with the staff and customers.

I had wanted to accompany Lamar to my father's place, but since Mason had his afternoon off, I needed to stay. Lamar assured me that if something occurred, he would call me. I didn't like it, but what could I do? My mate had asked me numerous times to sell the salon because it wasn't safe anymore. I, of course, had declined; The Cutting Edge Hair Salon was my baby. It was something that belonged to me. I had bought the place and turned it into what now was known as the place to go if you needed a decent haircut.

The day dragged on and didn't seem to come to an end. Finally, it was almost eight o'clock when I closed the salon. Milo had been with my grandparents; they adored my dog. I would drive straight to my father's estate because everyone would be there. Well, except for Eric and Liam. They stayed at my place. Liam didn't want to leave the safety of the home I shared with Lamar. Ralph and Justin had been visiting and would stay the night as well.

Our house was guarded by the Balashov Streak and the McLaughlin Pack soldiers. They should be safe. I walked into the living room and saw Dimitri standing behind Felix's chair. What was going on?

Milo came running, and I hugged him. "Hey boy, did you miss me?" I cooed. "There you are, Kotyonok," Grandma Natalya said, smiling, hugging me tightly. Even though she was my grandmother, the woman still had strength because she nearly squeezed the breath out of me. Dimitri observed the interaction between my Grandma Natalya and me intently.

I knew that Dimitri also had a long talk with Nicolay and Natalya Balashov, his parents, my grandparents. Dimitri had been sincere when he had apologized for his behavior and that he was done with Igor. He was genuinely happy to be accepted as a member of the Balashov Streak again.

I eyed the two hyenas and noticed that Felix had sought the nearness and protection of Dimitri. As far as I knew, Dimitri was straight, and he had a fiancé in Russia. So, what was going on? First, Arden told us that Titus, their former leader, planned to attack the tigers and the wolves. Then he had informed us that Igor was working with the Karr Brothers. Somehow Igor had gone berserk because he was planning on wiping out the entire Balashov Streak and the McLaughlin Pack as well.

Still, we didn't know why Igor was so hell-bent on planning full-out war; it was insane. It was unlikely that even with the help of the hyenas, Igor could win this battle. Arden and Felix told us where the hyenas had their headquarters and even where Titus lived. Granted, they had valuable information that could give us an advantage.

Arden's phone rang, and the hyena looked uncertain. "Take the call, and put, whoever it is, on speaker," my father said. Arden nodded as he swiped over the display. "Hey, David," Arden softly said. David Rendon was one of Titus' betas. "Arden? Is everything alright? Rumor is that you are taken by the tigers. Can you talk?" David had spoken softly. He knew that shifters had a superior hearing, and if Arden really had been kidnapped, then the tigers would hear the conversation.

"I'm in the company of the Balashov Streak and the McLaughlin Pack, but they didn't kidnap me," Arden began. He eyed my father, who nodded for him to continue, letting him know that he was doing okay. "What do you mean? Explain," he urged; it wasn't a command. David still used a soothing tone, which surprised me.

Arden looked at Felix, who nodded encouragingly to tell David the truth. "I'm not alone. Felix is with me as well. We asked the leader of the tigers for sanctuary, and Mr. Balashov granted it," Arden's voice had gone very low, barely audible. It was clear that the man was scared. It took a few minutes before David reacted, and it wasn't the reaction I had expected. "Did they force you to tell me this?" David asked. "No! They did not," Arden replied without missing a beat.

"Why? Why would you want to leave us?" David questioned, and he still didn't sound angry. "I wanted out because I'm sick and tired of the terror of which Titus and his brother are ruling the clan. David, we live in fear every single day, and I can't take it anymore," Arden sounded sincere. The shifter had told the truth; he really was fed up with the rain of terror that the Karr Brothers ruled the clan, as was Felix. The man hadn't said much, but then, he was the quiet one.

David was quiet for a long time, then he said in a soft voice, "You and me both." He paused, then he added, "Mr. Balashov? Can I talk to you, please?" I frowned, my father raised his eyebrows, Lamar looked suspicious, and Arkady scowled.

"Yes," he eyed Arden as he said, "Is it alright if I take your phone so that I can talk in private with David?" Arden looked shocked, but not for the reasons that we were thinking. "Of course, you are my master now," Arden softly said, with a trembling voice. My father took Arden's phone, then he looked at me, and I knew what to do.

"Arden, come with me, please?" I said in a soothing tone. Arden paled even more; the man was horrified. It made me wonder how much they had suffered at the hands of the Karr Brothers.

"There's no need to be afraid, Arden. I just want to explain a few things about how we, as a pack, or streak, or whatever, function," I softly said. I eyed Felix, who had gone very pale as well. "I want you to come too," I said. We went into the sunroom, where we had some privacy.

"I can only imagine how you must have suffered at the hands of Titus and his brother. We do things very differently here. My father asked you for your phone. You are allowed to refuse. Also, we don't believe in punishing members." I paused, eyed both hyenas, then I said, "The way I understand is that Titus rules his clan with an iron fist. Well, we don't. Every member has a right to their opinion."

"I don't understand," Felix whispered. I smiled reassuringly. "It means that you are allowed to speak your mind. If you don't like how things are, you can say so. Members of the Balashov Streak or the McLaughlin Pack are free to pursue their dreams," I explained. "As long as you show respect, you have the freedom to live life the way you want," I added.

There was a soft knock. "Enter Dimitri," I said, smiling. My uncle entered the sunroom and immediately crossed the room where Felix was sitting. "Is everything okay?" he gently questioned. "Yes, all is fine. Mr. Uh, Mitchell was explaining the rules," the hyena replied in a soft voice. They had addressed me as Mr. Balashov, and that wasn't right. So, I had urged both of them that the tigers and the wolves were on a first-name basis. Even my father and Lamar were addressed that way. I knew that it would take time for Arden and Felix to get used to this new life, but they would be fine.

Chapter 14

Dimitri's phone rang, and I saw the man's smile vanish. I frowned because who could it be that made Dimitri look so grim. He excused himself, and I watched the disappointment in Felix's eyes. What the hell was going on between Dimitri and Felix?

We went into the living room again, where my father was already waiting. He eyed Arden and Felix for a while, then he said, "David Rendon and Kent Acuna want to meet me." Arden cocked his head. Felix frowned. "Why do they want to meet," Arden whispered. "I'm not going back; I won't go back," Felix yelled as he ran into Dimitri's arms.

"No one is going back; you have my word," my father assured. Felix was about to have a full-blown panic attack. Dimitri gently stroked Felix's hair, whispering sweet nothings in the shifter's ear. To my astonishment, Felix did calm down. Could they be mates? Surely not because Dimitri was straight.

"David and Kent want to leave the clan," my father said. That got everyone's attention. "This could be a trap; you know that, right, dad?" I warned. "I'm aware of that, Mitchell. However, they sounded sincere, and I need to hear them out before I decide what to do," my father explained. That could only mean one thing, David and Kent would ask my father to grant them sanctuary.

I opened my mouth to tell my father that I didn't like it, but he shut me down. "I will take Dimitri and Arkady with me," he assured. And his tone let me know that it was final, with no room for discussion. "Can I?" "No! You can't, Mitchell," my father said.

"David and Kent are betas and enforcers as well. Titus loved to take us to his torture room, which we called the cellar. David and Kent had always been the ones who had to beat us to an inch of our lives. They never touched us, never harmed us in any way. If anything, they helped us many times by bringing food and blankets instead of beating us to a pulp." Arden said. "They really never touched us. In fact, they always had been nice," Felix insisted. My father nodded. "I will take that into consideration," he promised.

"So, you're not scared of them?" Eric gently questioned Felix. Felix shook his head. "No, not for Kent and David," he replied in a soft voice.

My father left, followed by Arkady and my Uncle Dimitri. Felix stared for a long time at the door. "They will be back before you know it," I said soothingly. Arden sat down next to Felix and put his arm around the smaller shifter's shoulder. He was reassuring his friend, which made him golden in my book. They were friends who would do anything to keep the other safe.

Two hours later, my father was back. "And?" I inquired. "David and Kent will arrive tomorrow morning. I granted them sanctuary," my father explained. I frowned. "That's it?" I was stunned. My father eyed me intently; he said, "Yes, that's it. You look surprised; why?" I opened my mouth to answer, but nothing came to mind, so I closed it again.

Tomorrow two betas slash enforcers would come to live with my father. I still didn't like the thought of that, but it had been my father's decision. My father, Alexei Balashov, was the leader of the tigers, so it had been his call to make.

While my father explained his decision regarding David and Kent, I noticed that Dimitri kept his distance from a very confused Felix. Had I missed something? Probably because I felt Felix's despair, which wasn't good. I sighed when Dimitri excused himself and went to his room. What the hell?

******

"Felix is gone," Arden yelled as he ran into the kitchen where I was sipping from my coffee. Lamar and I hadn't stayed at my father's estate for the night, but we had left for home. So now we were back again and drinking coffee and having breakfast. My grandmothers, yes, both, had insisted that we would join the family for breakfast. Of course, Lamar and I hadn't minded at all. Grandma Natalya and Grandma Anichka always cooked a fabulous breakfast.

I shot upright at hearing the panic and anger in Arden's voice. The panic I understood because his friend had disappeared in the middle of the night. The anger I couldn't place.

"Where is Dimitri, so I can kick his ass," he growled, and his eyes started glowing. Arden was about to shift, shit. Then, as if things couldn't get worse, Dimitri came into the kitchen. Lamar, get Arden out of here," I said. Lamar didn't hesitate because the tone of which I had spoken was enough to react immediately.

Dimitri looked surprised. "What's going on? Did I miss something?" he inquired. I shook my head. "I'm not sure," I said. "All I know is that Felix is gone; he disappeared during the night. Now, Arden is beside himself," I informed my uncle. Dimitri paled, and fear filled his eyes. Now I truly was confused. "Tell me what the hell is going on between you and Felix," I demanded.

"That's something I would like to know too," my father said as he sipped his coffee. Grandma Anichka, who was standing with her back to the stove, said, "He's your mate, right?" Dimitri didn't answer. I had guessed something like that, and it shouldn't come as a surprise, but it did.

"My fiancé called yesterday. She is on her way to Serigala Valley as we speak," he said matter of factly. "Your what?" I exclaimed because this was something I hadn't anticipated; the man had a fiancé? Lamar came into the kitchen again, followed by a now seemingly calm Arden who eyed Dimitri. "The man is your mate, and you ignored him. That's why he left," Arden whispered.

"I can only hope that Titus doesn't find him before we do," Arden said as he gave Dimitri a murderous look. "Shit," I grabbed my phone to let Jason know that I wouldn't come in today. "Scott and Simon are on their way," Lamar said as he put away his phone. "They are the pack's best trackers. If anyone can find Felix, it's Scott and Simon," I explained.

Simon and Scott did not come to the house but started searching in front of the wrought-iron gate. "He went that way," Simon said, pointing in the direction of the forest. "Damn, not the forest," Arden cursed. At the questioning look I gave him, Arden added, "That's Titus' hunting grounds." "Shit. We need to find him,' I urged. Simon and

Scott were already running toward the woods, following Felix's scent.

Dimitri stayed at the house, which surprised me, but now was not the time. I would ask for an explanation later. Right now, it was of utmost importance to find Felix before Titus did. However, if the forest was Titus' hunting grounds, then there was a chance that Titus had gotten to Felix. My blood ran cold at the thought of gentle, kind Felix at the mercy of that psychopath.

Simon had changed into his wolf, and Scott was running after him, and we were following them. Arden ran beside my father but couldn't keep up with the man. Simon ran even faster, and it became difficult to keep up. Then, Arden gasped and slowed; the man was staring at me, wide-eyed. "What's wrong?" I questioned while I kept running. Finally, Arden was beside me again but kept a distance between us.

"That's his second form. Keep running; we'll talk later," Lamar growled. And, to my delight, Arden listened because he began to run faster. Then, suddenly, Simon stopped, lifted his head, and howled. My heart nearly stopped beating; this wasn't good. I knew when a tracker or any other shifter found a dead pack member; they howled in grief.

"No," I whispered as I skidded to a halt. Arden looked at me in question. "Stay here," I commanded. But, of course, Arden didn't stay; he followed me to where a body was lying, partly buried under leaves. "NO," Arden screamed. Scott had done his best to keep Arden from seeing the body, but the shifter had managed nonetheless.

Titus had found Felix, and the man was dead. I could see that he was beaten badly. His face was swollen, and his arms and legs were twisted in unnatural angles. Felix's arms and legs were broken, they not only had beaten him, but they had tortured him to death. I can't describe the emotions that crossed my mind, body, and soul. Felix, kind and gentle Felix had been tortured to death. I couldn't believe it, hell, I didn't *want* to believe it.

Chapter 15

I sat in front of the floor-to-ceiling window, watching Dimitri. The man hadn't said a word since we had returned with Felix's body. Now, his fiancé had arrived at the airport and was on her way to Serigala Valley. What a fucking mess.

I turned when I felt Lamar enter the room, the doctor right behind him. "I can't make any promises. He's hanging on, but." "Felix is going to make it! He will be fine again," Arden said in a low voice that was full of emotions. Well, the man's best friend was in for the fight of his life. Unfortunately, Doctor Belinsky had said that Felix was severely wounded and probably wouldn't make it.

When we found him, Felix was barely alive. His heartbeat had slowed to the point that even we couldn't sense it anymore; that's why we thought that Felix was dead. Thank God that we had been wrong.

Grandma Anichka and grandma Natalya were working on healing potions and spells to give Felix the strength he needed to pull through. Not only was the hyena mortally wounded, but he didn't seem to fight. It seemed that he didn't want to live anymore.

"Felix should be fighting for his life right now. Yet, it seems that he has given up," I softly stated when Dimitri came into the room. He looked at me, and for a moment, I thought that he would say something, but he didn't. Instead, he walked out of the room, and I heard him going up the stairs. I shook my head; this was so not what I expected. Dimitri had to feel the mating pull. Yet, here he was, ignoring his dying mate, and for what?

The doorbell rang, which was strange because we didn't expect anyone. At a time like this, when everyone was on high alert, you needed to call before you were allowed to come to the house. It was just a precaution, but it worked. So, who could be ringing the doorbell like a mad person?

"Where is Dimitri?" my father asked. Next to him stood a woman. She wasn't stunning, but she was beautiful, kind of. However, her eyes were cold, and I instantly didn't like her. "In his room, probably," I shrugged. "Mitchell, meet Alyona Barinov, Dimitri's fiancé," my father introduced the woman. I stood and nodded, I didn't want to touch her, so I kept my distance. "Hello," I said before I turned, opened the sliding doors, and disappeared into the garden. I knew that I had been rude to the woman, but it was the way I felt. If I didn't like someone, I couldn't pretend that I liked that person.

"Are you alright, baby?" Lamar asked as he came to stand behind me and wrapped his strong arms around my shoulders. "No, I'm not alright," I softly replied. "Talk to me. Don't shut me out," Lamar gently insisted. "Felix is badly wounded; he might not make it. Dimitri is his mate, and he doesn't care. And now, Alyona Barinov, Dimitri's fiancé arrived out of the blue. Why did she come here? There's something about that woman that doesn't add up. I can't put my finger on it, but something isn't right," I said.

I was wondering what Alyona Barinov was doing in Serigala Valley. "Right now, Felix needs Dimitri, but he's not available because Alyona is here. This is so not what

Felix needs." I eyed my mate. " I'm scared," I admitted. Lamar frowned. "Scared of what, baby," my mate softly asked as he kissed me behind my ear, making me shiver.

"I'm scared that Felix might not make it because he lost the will to live. But, if you think that they hurt him physically, that's nothing compared to how Dimitri hurt his soul and broke his heart into a million pieces," I whispered. Dimitri has hurt Felix so much, I can feel his pain, literally feel it," I said.

"I want Alyona gone as soon as possible. If she stays, then it will kill Felix for sure," I said. Lamar sighed; he said, "You need to talk to your father; tell him what you told me." "I intend to," I said. Together we stood for some time, just enjoying being close. I wanted to leave the house for a while, but I didn't want to leave Felix. But then, there was Arden; he would start a fight with Dimitri as soon as he saw the shifter. I couldn't blame him because I would have done the same.

I looked at Lamar. "Is there any news about the murder investigation that you are currently working on?" I asked. My mate was still investigating the murder of Elijah Reed, Dusty's son. With so much going on, I didn't have the chance to ask him about it.

"Not really. We have no witnesses, no clues, and no motive. I only know that the scent of hyenas was still present when I arrived at the scene. That and I sensed the smell of tiger, and it wasn't Igor." Lamar paused, inhaled deeply, then he continued.

"I guess that Igor had some of his followers hunt Liam down, but somehow they ended up killing Elijah. Liam and Elijah do look a lot like each other despite the age difference." Lamar stared deep into my eyes. "It's frustrating as hell," he softly added. I wrapped my arms around his waist and let my head rest against his back. "I know that you will solve the case. You're a good detective, and you have good instincts," I told him, and it wasn't because he was my mate. Lamar was an excellent detective, and his hunches had always been right. When Lamar's gut instinct let him know that something was off, then it was.

"What do you want to do about Alyona Barinov?" Lamar questioned as we sat down on the lounge chairs on the back deck. "You believe me that something doesn't add up. That she can't be trusted?" I asked. "I sure do. You aren't a detective, but you also have good instincts," he said. I smiled. Yes, I had the best, kindest and sexiest mate in the universe.

"You could check her out, do some kind of background check. After all, there's still a lot of family members that would help you gather information," Lamar suggested. I raised my eyebrows because the man was right. "Why haven't I thought of that?" "Because I'm a genius?" Lamar laughed. I laughed too.

Suddenly there was yelling, and it came from inside the house. "Shit! Arden and Dimitri, God damn," I cursed as I ran inside, Lamar hot on my heels. Sure enough, Arden and Dimitri stood almost nose to nose. They would have fought, but my father was fast as he squeezed himself between the two. "Stop it, both of you," he commanded, and to my relief, they stopped yelling. Alyona watched from afar, and I couldn't help but notice that she was smiling. It was a dirty smile; she was enjoying herself, that bitch.

"Calm down, baby. Your eyes are glowing," Lamar warned. "I'm going to check on Felix," I said because I had to get away from that evil woman. Yes, I was convinced that she was evil, pure evil.

I took the stairs, two at the time, and softly knocked before I slightly opened the door. Doctor Belinsky was replacing one of the IVs but motioned for me to come in, which I did. Felix was small for a shifter, and he looked even smaller, lying there in that huge bed. He looked so pale, and I felt his pain. "He's in pain, even though he's unconscious," I informed Doctor Belinsky. The doctor frowned. "That shouldn't be possible. I have special meds to prevent him from feeling any kind of pain," the doctor replied.

"Well, I can feel not only his physical pain, but the hurt he feels inside, in his heart, and his soul," I explained. The doctor looked thoughtful; he said, "Felix is not making any progress." Doctor Belinsky eyed me, and then he softly said, "If it goes on like this, then Felix won't make it."

I sighed deeply because I knew that he was right. "Dimitri doesn't acknowledge Felix as his mate. In fact, his fiancé is here because she misses him so much, which is bullshit," I growled as my blood began to boil again. "Control yourself, Kotyonok." I turned and saw Grandma Natalya standing in the doorway.

She looked at the doctor. "How is Felix doing?" she asked. Doctor Belinsky shook his head; he said, "Not good, he's not making any progress. There's only so much I can do; the rest would be up to Felix."

"Felix has lost the will to live; he doesn't fight for his life because Dimitri has denied him as his mate. Felix knows this, even though he's unconscious," I softly said. "We have a potion ready, but it won't help him. Felix needs the will to live, to fight for what's his," Grandma Anichka whispered. "He looks so small, so fragile," she added. I saw tears in her eyes.

"I'll be right back. I need to speak to Dimitri," I said as I rushed out of the room. The words of my grandmother echoed in my mind. Felix needs to fight for what's his. Dimitri was Felix's mate, goddammit. So he needed to get angry so that the healing could start, physically and emotionally. Felix's body and soul needed to start healing, or he wouldn't make it. The thought of Felix dying because of Dimitri filled me with rage. I felt my tiger stir; the animal was even more enraged than I was. Shit, I took a few deep breaths and managed to keep my tiger under control.

Chapter 16

"What the hell?" Dimitri growled as I burst into his room. Alyona was with him; she sat on the bed, staring daggers at me. Well, let her be angry; I couldn't care less. "What is the meaning of this?" Alyona demanded to know. I ignored her and spoke directly to Dimitri; it was now or never. Whatever happened, I couldn't, wouldn't let Felix die, not without a fight.

"Can I talk to you?" I glanced at Alyona. "In private?" I added while I kept glaring at the bitch. I could tell that she was not amused; in fact, she was getting angry. Well, tough luck! Dimitri looked at his fiancé. "Don't look at her," I growled. The growl seemed to bring Dimitri back to the here and now again. He eyed Alyona and said in a tone that left no room for argument, "Leave us. Mitchell and I have things to discuss."

If looks could have killed me, I would have dropped dead right that second. As it was, I wasn't impressed by her attitude; she was a stupid bitch. "But Dimitri, you can't send me away like you do a servant," Alyona protested. I glanced at Dimitri, and the man got the message. "I believe that I just did," he replied coolie. I smiled inwardly; it was a big smile because now I knew Dimitri cared about Felix. My heart was skipping a beat or two because I was so happy.

"Leave, now," Dimitri said, and this time he didn't sound very friendly. Alyona scowled, but she finally stood and left the room, ignoring both of us. "I know what it is that you want to talk about, but tell me anyway," my uncle said, looking expectantly at me. "I'm here to tell you that Felix, your fated mate, is dying."

Dimitri paled; he looked genuinely shocked. Hadn't he known how bad Felix was doing? "Tell me," he whispered. So, I did. I told him that Felix was hurt so badly by Dimitri's rejection that the shifter had lost the will to live. For his body to heal, his emotional scars needed to heal first. Those two are connected; the one doesn't function without the other, I explained.

Dimitri swallowed hard. "He thought that I denied him as my mate?" he softly said. I nodded. "It wasn't that I denied him, but. Shit, what a mess." Dimitri had his head in his hands. Then, he looked up. "Tell me, what can I do to save his life. I know that he's my mate. And believe it or don't, but I need him," Dimitri whispered.

I told him about the potions my Grandmothers Anichka and Natalya had ready but that they wouldn't help as long as Felix didn't start fighting. "Go, and sit with him. Tell him how you feel and that you need him," I urged. "I will, but you need to prevent Alyona from coming anywhere near Felix." Dimitri eyed me, then he whispered, "She is dangerous, don't underestimate her," he warned. I promised to keep Alyona away from Felix just as long as he spent time with his mate.

"One more thing," I said. Dimitri stared at me. "Yes?" "Did you know that Alyona was coming to Serigala Valley?" I questioned. Dimitri shook his head. "No, I did not. She never mentioned that she wanted to come too," he answered without missing a beat. That was good enough for me. Then, another thought came to mind. "Why would you marry someone who wasn't your mate?" I inquired because it was something I really didn't understand.

Dimitri sighed. "I didn't want to marry her, and not only because she's not my fated mate. I don't even like her," he confessed. That had me even more confused. "Then, why?" "Igor urged me to marry Alyona because it was the best thing to do. She would provide cubs to secure the Balashov line," he answered.

I couldn't believe what I was hearing. "That bastard!" I growled. "Well said. I fell for it with open eyes. I can't believe that I was so stupid, so naive," Dimitri softly said. "Well, the main thing is that you love Felix, your true mate. That you don't love that bitch, Alyona. So, now we can throw her out of the house," I grinned because that would be so nice seeing her face when I would kick her to the curb.

I didn't know where Alyona had gone; no one had seen her, which was disturbing.
I needed to know where she was now, more than ever. I was sure that she would pose a danger to Felix because the shifter was Dimitri's fated mate. We really needed Alyona out of the house as quickly as possible. Since no one knew where she was, I couldn't kick her out yet.

"So, my brother finally acknowledged Felix as his mate?" my father said, but he didn't look happy. We were in the sunroom, drinking coffee. Dimitri had gone upstairs to see Felix. I knew that the shifter would feel Dimitri's presence and his devotion. I hoped now that Dimitri showed his love and adoration, Felix would start fighting, that he would want to live again.

"You're not pleased. Why not?" I questioned because it confused me. The man should be ecstatic about the fact that Dimitri had chosen for his mate, and not that bitch,

Alyona. "It might be too late," my father whispered. "No, surely not," I said. My father didn't reply, and that worried me.

"Now that Dimitri has chosen Felix, he must start fighting for his life. I mean, Felix must feel Dimitri's presence, right? Felix had too much to live for; he can't give up now," I whispered and prayed that it wasn't too late.

"Now that Dimitri has chosen Felix, your grandmothers will start administering the potions they brew with the spells that they wrote. After that, it's up to Felix," my father informed me.

I wanted to go upstairs to see how Felix was doing, but my father stopped me. He said, "The doctor, Dimitri, and your grandmothers are with Felix right now. Too many people in the room could cause stress."

Suddenly we heard raised voices coming from the hall entrance. We went into the hall to see what the commotion was all about. "What's going on?" my father questioned, and his tone wasn't friendly. "I demand to see my fiancé," Alyona shrieked. I wanted to give her a piece of my mind, but again, my father stopped me.

He eyed Alyona intently, then said in a voice that even gave me the creeps. "Dimitri isn't available right now. You have to wait. And furthermore, do not use that tone with any of my family members ever again. You are in my house, so show some respect!"

Alyona looked shocked; it was evident that no one had ever spoken to her like my father just had done. She stared daggers at me; it was apparent that she didn't like me. "What he said," I pointed at my father, smiling.

Alyona opened and closed her mouth several times. She looked like a fish, but I better not tell her that because it would probably set her off all over again. She looked uncertain for a short moment; then, she lifted her head and headed for the stairs. But, before we could stop her, she burst into Felix's room. Shit, that was so not what Felix or Dimitri needed right now.

"What the hell are you doing in here?" Alyona shrieked. My grandmothers, doctor Belinsky, and Dimitri all stared at her. They weren't friendly stares either. Felix stirred, and it looked like he was in pain. I closed my eyes, and then I knew that the shifter was in pain. It wasn't physical pain; no, Felix was suffering, mentally.

Alyona, who apparently just had noticed that Dimitri held Felix's hand, looked shocked. "Don't you touch him. Don't you dare touch him. I'm your fiancé, and you will marry me," Alyona shrieked. Felix stirred more violently this time. I glanced at my father and saw that Lamar had joined us. *"We need to get that bitch out of the room. Felix is reacting to her presence, and not in a good way,"* I used our mind link to inform my mate so that he could remove Alyona by surprise.

We didn't need her to shriek and yell even more because it wasn't good for Felix. Lamar nodded, and before Alyona could react, he had her out of the room. Dimitri nodded in thanks. It was a relief to know that Dimitri was going for Felix, lock, stock, and barrel.

It took a long time before Lamar returned as he motioned for my father and me to follow him. Shit, this wasn't good. "I managed to calm her down, somewhat. But she won't give up. That woman is hell bend on marrying Dimitri, and God only knows why. By now, it's clear that he doesn't want her. Hell, didn't he tell you he doesn't even like her?" It was apparent that Lamar was outraged.

"Oh, and I told her to book a hotel, and I'll send the baggage there," Lamar informed us. "How did she take it?" I inquired. Lamar frowned, he said, "Not good, as you surely can imagine. I think that it's not the last time that we've heard of Alyona Barinov," he added.

He was probably right. "Well, she better not try and harm Felix because, woman or not, then she will have to answer to me," I said. "Then she will need to answer to all of us," my father said. Lamar nodded his approval. I smiled because we would protect each other; it was what family did.

Chapter 17

"I can't believe it. This is insane. What was she thinking? Her family is filthy rich, so she doesn't need the money. I don't understand." "Baby, stop!" Lamar softly said. I stared at Lamar. "Shit, I was rambling, wasn't I?" "Yes, baby, you were," my mate replied. "Sorry," I apologized.

After Lamar had kicked out Alyona, she had called to let him know at which hotel she would be staying. So, Lamar had packed her things and had sent them to the hotel. But, he also had sent two of the pack members to that same hotel to keep an eye on her. My mate didn't trust her; well, neither of us did. So, I was glad that he had Alyona under surveillance.

Adam and Billy were at the hotel, and they had the brilliant idea to book the room next to Alyona's. It was the perfect way to eavesdrop. The moment she entered the room, Alyona had immediately called someone. Because the hotel room walls were so thin, Billy and Adam had heard the complete conversation between Alyona and the man she was talking to.

"I want Dimitri in here as well because he needs to know what Alyona has done," my father looked grim, and rightly so. "I'll see if he can leave Felix for a while," Lamar said as he headed for the stairs. My grandmothers Anichka and Natalya looked somber; my grandfather looked like he could kill Alyona. He probably would, too, if he got the chance.

"What is so urgent that I had to leave my mate?" Dimitri questioned. I was pleased to see Dimitri so devoted to Felix. "You better sit down, Dimitri," my father softly said. Dimitri frowned, then his expression changed into worry. He sat down and looked intently at my father. "Your friend, Gregor Ivanov, is very sick. Did you know?" my father began carefully. "I know, yes. Gregor is very sick," Dimitri replied.

Gregor Ivanov was one of Dimitri's best friends, and the man was human. He was fifty-five years, so not particularly old for a human. Still, the man was very sick, dying, in fact. "Gregor has cancer; he's on borrowed time," Dimitri said, and he looked so sad that it broke my heart.

"But what about him?" Dimitri questioned. My father sighed. I could tell that it was difficult for him to tell his brother what was going on. To inform his brother what Alyona had done and why.

"Did you know that you are the sole beneficiary of Gregor's fortune?" Dimitri's eyes grew wide with astonishment. He hadn't known; that much was obvious. "I didn't know. How?" "It doesn't matter. What matters right now is that you know what's going on with Alyona. What that bitch did."

When Dimitri didn't say anything, my father continued. "When Lamar kicked Alyona out of the house, she let him know the hotel she was staying at. Lamar needed to know so he could send her belongings there. Lamar had immediately sent Adam and Billy to the hotel to keep an eye on her. They booked a room next to Alyona's. That's when they overheard Alyona's conversation with an unknown male. They talked about poisoning Gregor.

That's why he is dying of cancer; Alyona poisoned him."
My father paused, giving Dimitri time to digest everything.

Dimitri had gone very pale, and my heart was breaking
for the man. "You didn't know that you would inherit
everything, but Alyona did. That's why she poisoned
Gregor and wants to marry you. But, then, she probably
would murder you to get her hands on all the money, your
own fortune, and that of Gregor." The silence was
deafening.

Dimitri was visibly upset. It was evident that he hadn't
anticipated that Alyona could be so devious. Then
Dimitri's eyes began to glow; yep, the man was livid. "She
murdered Gregor, so I'm going to kill her. A life for a life,"
Dimitri said in a too calm voice. "Alyona's life is forfeit,"
my father said. It meant so much as go ahead and kill that
bitch. Well, it was Dimitri's right.

Since Alyona was a shifter, she had to obey their law,
and she had taken a life for no other reason than greed. She
had taken a human life at that, which was unforgivable,
and Dimitri was in his right to end her existence.

I knew that if it were up to my father, he would have
searched for another solution than to kill Alyona, but it was
what it was. I was surprised that I didn't have second
thoughts about killing Alyona. I guess that it was a sign
that I was getting more and more used to being a shifter. I
prayed that I wouldn't lose my humanity because it was
who I was. I had lived as a human for most of my life, and
it had made me the man I was today.

The doorbell chimed, and my father stood to see who it
was. He returned a moment later, a manilla envelope in his
hands. "For you," he said as he handed me the envelope. I

frowned because I didn't expect mail. I sat down and tore the envelope open. The contents shocked the hell out of me. Inside were pictures of Elijah Reed, the mutilated body of Elijah Reed.

"What's wrong, baby?" Lamar asked in alarm. My head was spinning, and my blood began to boil, literally boil. "Shit, call Doctor Belinsky," I heard my father yell. Then, my world went black.

When I opened my eyes again, I was in my father's bedroom. "What happened?" A moment later, I remembered, and I groaned. "No no no. Where is the envelope?" I needed to know because no one should see what was inside.

"It's inside of my desk, under lock and key," my father answered, and judging by his and Lamar's expressions, they had seen the pictures too. "There's also a letter inside the envelope. We didn't read it, though," Lamar said. I knew why they hadn't read the letter because it was addressed to me. "I need to see the pictures and the letter," I said.

My father nodded before he left the room to get the envelope. Even though it had been shocking, I needed to study the pictures. We needed to know if they were real. Plus, I needed to know what was in that letter. I hadn't seen it because my system had crashed when I saw the horrible pictures of Elijah's mutilated body.

I got out of bed and went into the bathroom to splash some water on my face. I wasn't looking forward to seeing those pictures again. As it was, I didn't have a choice. Grandma Anichka had told me that as a shifter, Vera Reed had felt her young son's pain while he was tortured. So, that the woman had snapped and seemed catatonic wasn't a surprise.

Lamar was still investigating Elijah's murder, but he had hit wall after wall after wall. The delivery of the envelope could mean a turning point. Well, one could only hope. I took the envelope from the coffee table and pulled the photos and the letter out. I put the pictures aside and started reading the letter.

******

To Mitchell

The pictures are real, unfortunately. The murder of Elijah Reed wasn't a mix-up. It was Igor who ordered the kill because Elijah came too close. The young tracker had just found out where Igor's hiding place was when Igor got to him. I don't know why Igor didn't touch Elijah, but he let Titus do his dirty work.

Well, you know how it ended. I tried to rescue Elijah, but they got to me too. I barely escaped, but not before they tortured me, nearly killing me in the process.

I'm so sorry that Elijah wasn't that fortunate because I really liked him. I managed to take those horrible pictures of poor Elijah before they captured me as well.

I can't reveal my identity because even though I survived Igor's, well, treatment, I didn't escape unharmed.

I am writing you this letter because I just wanted to let you know that Titus murdered Elijah, but Igor ordered it. So it wasn't a mix-up. It wasn't supposed to be Liam.

****

I blinked a few times because, what the hell? I handed the letter to my father. Lamar had read it simultaneously with me as he stood behind me. "Do you believe the one who wrote this?" my father questioned. I nodded. "I do because I have no reason to believe otherwise," I replied. "Then we need to find out who wrote the letter," Lamar said.

"I agree, but this person is terrified of Igor. And, if it's true, then he's still suffering from the torture Igor put him through," I said. My father sighed; Lamar frowned as I took the pictures of the table and studied them intently. It wasn't a pretty sight, but it was the only lead we had so far.

I took the magnifying glass and concentrated not on the mutilated body of Elijah but on the surroundings. That's when I saw it. "Look," I said as I pointed to the barely visible arm. I knew that wristwatch, and apparently, so did Lamar and my father. "Titus Karr," my father and Lamar growled simultaneously. Even though I shouldn't have been surprised at hearing that name, I was. I didn't need to ask if they were sure about Titus Karr. "So, what does that tell us?" I said.

"It tells us that Igor and Titus still are working together. Maybe they still do, I don't know. But now we have reason to attack the hyenas and kill Titus and his brother," Lamar said. "How can you know that Travis is involved as well?" I questioned. "Titus doesn't do anything without his deranged brother. You must know that Travis is even more disturbed than Titus," my father explained.

Chapter 18

"I want him to suffer before he dies," Dusty's voice was so low and so menacing that it gave even me the creeps. "And he will," my mate promised. "By my hand," Dusty growled. Again, my mate agreed.

After studying the photos and analyzing the letter, we decided it was real. That meant that we needed to inform Dusty about it. As expected, the man had almost lost it, and now he was on the warpath, which was his good right. After all, Igor and the Karr brothers had not only killed Dusty's son; they had slaughtered the boy. Those monsters had tortured Elijah until the boy had died. It would have taken a long time before the boy had taken his last breath. Shifters didn't die that easily.

"How is Vera holding up?" my father softly inquired. Dusty looked pained. "Not so good. She doesn't sleep, eat or talk. It's like she lost the connection to not only me but to the world," he paused. My father looked at me, and I saw the same pain in my father's eyes. Even though Dusty and Vera were wolf shifters, my father felt for them.

I gently squeezed my father's shoulder in silent support. I knew that the memories of the past were still haunting him. Well, we still were searching for my mother. But, I knew that if we found Igor, we would find my mother. I didn't doubt that for one moment.

I also knew that if we captured Igor, I would make him talk. According to my father, Igor was a hard one to crack. Well, I had learned some tricky spells, and I knew how to brew the truth serum. The serum would mash his brain, but

I couldn't care less. I would give Igor the chance to tell us where he had hidden my mother. If he refused, I would use the spell and the truth serum.

We had decided that Dusty would decide what to do with the Karr brothers. It was his right since they had participated in the torture and death of his only child. Doctor Belinsky entered the room. Dusty looked from Lamar to the doctor and then back to Lamar again.

"I suggested that the doctor should come by because you need to hear what he has to say," Lamar softly said. For a moment, it seemed as if Dusty would bolt, but then he nodded. "Are you willing to hear me out before you walk?" asked the doctor. Dusty was reluctant, but then he nodded.

"Vera doesn't respond to any kind of treatment. In fact, she's getting worse with every day that passes." Doctor Belinsky paused. "I know that. If it goes on like this, I don't think she will survive. I mean, she needs to eat and to get some sleep, right?" Dusty whispered.

Doctor Belinsky nodded. "I might have a solution, but it will be getting intense," he said while he eyed Dusty intently. "I have a feeling that I'm not going to like what you have to say," a somber-looking Dusty said. Doctor Belinksy pressed his lips together. He knew he was going to ask the nearly impossible from Dusty. "I would like to admit Vera. The Hope Garden Psychiatric Institution is excellent and for shifters only," said Doctor Belinsky in a careful voice.

All eyes were on Dusty, who obviously felt uncomfortable. "I don't know if she can manage without me. We've never been separated and." Dusty was too emotional to go on. Then he looked at Doctor Belinsky. "Could I see the place before I decide?" he asked in a soft voice. "Of course, you can. It's what a good mate would do. You are supposed to check out the place before you either consent or refuse the admittance of your mate," said Doctor Belinsky.

"I would love to tell you that Vera could be helped by giving her some medication, but that's not the case. Her pain and suffering are nestled deep inside her heart and soul. The Hope Garden Psychiatric Institution would be the perfect place for Vera. Doctor Krause is one of the best psychiatrists that I know. If anyone can bring Vera back from the deep dark, it's him," explained Doctor Belinsky. "You think about it, Dusty. I'm going to check on Felix," said the doctor.

"Would you accompany me to this institution? Mitchell?" I must admit that Dusty's request caught me off guard. "Yes, absolutely," I said. Doctor Belinsky had called Doctor Krause and dusty, and I could come and see him right away.

Doctor Belinsky wouldn't accompany us to The Hope Garden Psychiatric Institution because Felix needed him. Yesterday the young shifter's condition had been slightly improving, but today it seemed that Felix had a relapse, which was strange. Now that Dimitri had acknowledged Felix as his mate, the shifter should start recovering. No such luck; Felix had even fallen back into unconsciousness.

"And? What do you think?" Doctor Krause asked after he had shown us the facility. "I must admit that it's not what I expected," Dusty said as we sat down in Doctor Krause's office. "You thought that the rooms would be small and dark, right?" the doctor said. Dusty nodded, and

I must admit that it wasn't exactly what I had expected either.

The rooms were light and very spacious, the ones on the first floor had a small patio, and the rooms on the second floor had a balcony. The dining room was beautifully decorated in light yellow tones. It was like the sun shone all the time, even if it was cloudy outside.

Vera would get a room with light green tones because green was supposed to have a calming effect. After a long conversation with Doctor Krause, Dusty gave his consent to admit Vera. I felt the man's pain when he spoke the words.

Vera didn't resist when she was admitted; it told me how bad it really was. She just didn't care anymore. She didn't react when I kissed her cheek. Hell, she didn't even react when Dusty took her into his arms and kissed her goodbye. It was heartbreaking.

I wanted Dusty to stay with Lamar and me for the time being. He shouldn't be alone right now. Also, we didn't know where Igor was or what he was up to, which was concerning. And who was the person who had sent us the pictures of Elijah and written a letter telling us about Igor and the Karr Brothers?

"It's too bad that Igor isn't a wizard, or part wizard because then we could scry for him," said Grandma Natalya. "I can't wait to get my hands on that bastard," I said. "It's time that we find him," Lamar said. "No word on the streets?" I asked because Lamar had his people everywhere. "No, nothing. It's like Igor has gone up in smoke," my grim-looking mate replied.

"He's near; I can feel it," I said suddenly. Now, where had that come from? How do you know?" my father inquired. I opened my mouth but then closed it again because I didn't know how to answer. I simply didn't know how I knew that Igor was near. It was bizarre.

"Are you sure?" Lamar questioned. I nodded because I was too stunned to answer. "Baby?" Lamar said, and his tone was strangely urgent. "Come, sit down," Lamar took my arm and guided me to the chair in front of the window. It was my favorite chair.

"You're looking funny. Why are you looking at me like that?" I said. Lamar was scrutinizing me, and I didn't like it. "There's something going on with you. It's like, I don't know. "He's gaining power," I heard Grandma Anichka saying. That was the last thing I heard. I have no recollection after that.

I woke in bed. I was, once again, in my father's bedroom. "What the hell?" I cursed. "Lie down, baby. Please?" my mate urged. I didn't understand but did as I was told. After all, Lamar was my mate. "How are you feeling?" he asked as he sat on the edge of the bed and held my hand.

"What happened?" I inquired because something must have happened for me to land in my father's bedroom, again. "We're not sure. According to your grandmothers, you're gaining in power. What powers exactly, they don't know," Lamar paused; he eyed me intently. "What? Did I sprout two heads? You're looking at me funny," I said. "That's just it, you don't look different, but somehow, you do," my mate tried to explain. I frowned because, to me, Lamar didn't make any sense.

There was a soft knock, and Grandmothers Anichka and Natalya walked in. "You're glowing slightly, Kotyonok," Grandma Natalya said, smiling. "That's it. You are glowing, but it's so subtle that I didn't recognize it," Lamar said as he gently squeezed my hand.

The two women looked at each other, then both nodded and smiled. They looked, well, relieved. "Care to share," I asked. "Of course," said Grandma Anichka. "We know the gift that you got," said Grandma Natalya.

"Alright, can you please tell me what gift I received?" I knew that I sounded irritated, but I couldn't help it. "The gift of healing," both women said simultaneously. "The what? I don't understand. Does that mean that I'm a doctor now?"

Grandma Anichka shook her head. "No, but you should be able to help Felix," Grandma Natalya informed me. That got my full attention because there was nothing I'd wanted more than to see Felix healthy again. I swung my legs over the edge of the bed and immediately felt the dizziness nearly knocking me out.

"Easy, baby. Let me help you," Lamar said. My two grandmothers looked worried. Grandma Anichka said, "You should stay in bed, at least for the next couple of hours." "and how are we going to manage that?" my mate chuckled. He was right; I wouldn't have stayed in bed if my life depended on it. Felix and Dimitri needed me right now.

Chapter 19

As it was, my father summoned me before I could get to Felix's room. Doctor Belinsky was with him; this wasn't a good sign. "How is Felix doing?" I asked even though I dreaded the doctor's answer. Doctor Belinsky shook his head; he said, "Yesterday, Felix was progressing perfectly. Today not so much. He's lost consciousness again, and I don't know why that happened. Felix should be sitting upright in bed right now, cuddling with his mate. It's like he had a major setback overnight. I can't explain to you what even I don't understand," the doctor softly said.

"How are you?" the doctor inquired. "I'm fine. In fact, I'm doing great," I answered. I told my father and the doctor about what my two grandmothers had explained about the gift I had received. Doctor Belinsky frowned because he was confused. He had never heard of someone receiving a gift like that.

"Is it alright if I take a look at Felix?" I asked. Doctor Belinsky agreed, we went upstairs to Felix's room. I had asked how to use my gift because I was at a loss. Both my grandmothers had explained that it would come to me. That I automatically would know how to use my gift.

I slowly stepped closer to the bed. Then I saw it. "What the hell?" I softly cursed. No one said anything. Lamar had explained to Dimitri that I was there to help Felix. The shifter had consented because by now, he was desperate, which was understandable.

As I stepped closer, I didn't immediately recognize what it was that I was seeing. I concentrated, and then it slowly formed in my head. Felix was surrounded by some sort of magical barrier. I didn't have another word for it. I tried to penetrate the dark gray mass, but it wouldn't budge.

"Kotyonok?" I turned and saw that Grandmother Natalya motioned for me to come to her. "What is it?" I said. "You need to open up for your gift. Feel, smell, know," she said. "The way you approached Felix, it was like you were using a sledgehammer. I felt it. Your Grandmother Anichka felt it. I believe that even your mate felt it. You used aggression, which doesn't help," she gently explained.

"What should I do?" I asked. "As I said, open up, embrace whatever it is that you're facing," she instructed. I inhaled deeply, and then I was ready for a second try. This time I did what Grandma Natalya had told me to do.

I concentrated on the thick gray mass and gently started pushing it aside. At first, nothing happened. Then, it slowly vanished. It was like a fog that slowly dissolved. I didn't know how long it had taken me before the gray fog had disappeared entirely, but I felt drained.

"I can't believe it. You did it. Mitchell, you freaking did it," Dimitri whispered. I opened my eyes and saw that Felix was awake and smiling. "I did it," I whispered. Dimitri was hugging and kissing Felix, who enjoyed the attention his mate gave him.

We left the room to give them some privacy. I knew that my father and the others were anxious to hear my explanation. So, I told them about my gift. That now I had the ability to heal people or shifters. Everyone complimented me on how I had healed Felix. I didn't want compliments because it was a given that I had used my gift to heal the young shifter. "Well, I had help," I said as I eyed both of my grandmothers.

My father stood, rubbed his hands, and said, "We need to celebrate that Felix is on his way to recovery. Plus, my brother has accepted Felix as his fated mate." My father's smile was radiant. Even though Felix was awake, he still wasn't entirely healed. He would need time to recover completely. But, he and Dimitri would join us for a celebration meal.

My father had invited Andrei, his mate Katarina, and their son, Yuri, and of course, Vadim. Arkady would be joining us as well. He had Milo for the day, and I still was a bit baffled about Arkady adoring Milo. The first few times, Arkady had ignored my dog. Now, he loved Milo.

Ralph and Justin would come by and celebrate with us. And of course, my grandparents would be celebrating with us too. That made another thought surface, my grandfather Borya Vasiliev. He had been missing for a little over thirty years now. One day he had gone fishing, and the man had never returned. Grandma Anichka must miss her mate so much. The Vasiliev Family hadn't declared the shifter dead but assumed he must have died. Borya would have never left his mate. He loved and adored Anichka.

My father had told me about Grandfather Borya Vasiliev, but I wasn't convinced that the man was dead. I don't know how I knew, but my gut feeling let me know that my Grandfather was still alive. If he really was, then where was he? Why hadn't he returned to his mate? So many questions and no answers, it was something that could drive me mad. Maybe if you captured Igor, we would find out more about my grandfather Borya.

"We need to find Igor, and fast because we need answers only he can give us," I said. My father and my Uncles Andrei and Vadim were in the room with me. It was amazing how they had welcomed me into the Balashov family after my father had convinced them that I really was Mitchell Balashov. "You know that Igor is a tough one, right? You probably won't get him to spill the beans," my Uncle Vadim said. I smiled, and I knew that it wasn't a pleasant smile. I said, "I have my way to let him sing like a canary. Igor will tell me everything I want to know."

My Uncle Andrei eyed me for a moment. "Remind me not to get on your bad side," he said, and the man wasn't joking. "He took my mother from me. She has been deprived of watching her son grow up. He placed with the family from hell. My mother still is missing. My rage is growing with each passing day," I was whispering now because if I didn't, I would have screamed. No, I would have roared. "We will get him, eventually," my father said. "I know that we will," I replied.

Grandma Anichka, Grandma Natalya, my father, and Lamar would cook the celebration dinner. I set the table with Yuri, my nephew, who I had saved from drowning. I had left the engagement party from Liam's sister, and while I walked through the park, I had heard someone scream for help. When I saw that someone was about to drown, I hadn't hesitated. I jumped into the pond and dragged him onto the grass. It was when I had met my father for the first time. Well, I didn't know that he was my father, but my Grandmother, who was with him, had known.

"I knew right away who you were." I looked up. "What?" I asked because I thought that I had heard it wrong. Yuri smiled as he said, "That day, you saved me from drowning. I knew right away who you were." "How?" Yuri shrugged. "I don't know. But, I was sure, just as Grandmother Natalya. She knew it the minute you stepped into that pet store.

"I told my father who you were, but he didn't believe me right away. Only when I insisted that you were the real deal, he started to believe me," Yuri explained. "Do you always go through the park without Milo?" Yuri asked. I wanted to say, sure. But now that I thought about it, I knew that it wasn't true. I never walked through the park without Milo.

"Now that you mention it, no, I never go through the park if Milo's not with me. How did you know?" I questioned. "That's just something that I knew. I can't explain how, but I just know these things," Yuri softly said. "Does your father know?" I inquired. Yuri looked sat when he said, "No, he doesn't know." "Why not? You're not afraid of your father, right?" If so, then I would talk to my father about that.

Yuri shook his head vigorously. "No, absolutely not. It's just, well, he wouldn't understand." "Why wouldn't he understand? The man is a shifter," I replied. I was amazed that Andrei seemed to be so short-minded. He was a shifter, so he should be open to what he considered were strange things.

"What about your mother?" "She knows, and she tells me that it's a gift. And how precious I am to her and my father. But that my dad needs time to get used to having a

119

son who is special," Yuri said. I didn't have a reply because what could I say? Also, it was something that Uncle Andrei had to deal with, not me. After we set the table, Yuri and I headed for the living room. Liam stood, came toward me, and hugged me something fierce. "How are you?" he asked. "I should ask you that," I chuckled.

Liam was doing fine, and he and Eric had long talks about the shifter community and mates. Liam had come to trust Eric, and they seemed cozy, which was good. We all sat down, and a feeling of contentment flowed into my heart when I looked at all the people sitting at the table. My family and friends had gathered, and they enjoyed themselves. Katarina Bezrukov Balashov, Yuri's mother and Andrei's mate, sat to my left and Lamar to my right. The table was round, so there was no head of the table.

Everyone ate and drank and talked to each other. It really was a celebration dinner. Suddenly the hairs on the back of my neck stood on end. I touched Lamar lightly. *"Igor is here; I think that he is even on the premises,"* I told Lamar through the mind link we shared. Yuri had noticed something because he eyed me strangely. I smiled reassuringly at the boy, but he didn't buy it.

Thank God that dinner was finished, so Lamar and I could leave the table without raising suspicion. Well, my father wasn't fooled, and neither were my uncles and grandparents. Their reaction made the rest react as well.

"What's going on?" Liam asked, and he had gotten very pale. "He's here, isn't he?" Liam said, and it wasn't a question. I never lied to my friends, and I wouldn't start now. So, I said, "I believe so. We will check the premises. Eric will stay here so he can keep you safe." Dimitri stayed as well because he wanted to keep Felix safe. After all,

Igor still claimed that Felix was his rightful mate, which was bullshit.

So Ralph, and Justin, who were also present, would be safe because Dimitri and Eric would kill everyone who would try to harm the humans and Felix and Arden.

I would have liked it if Arkady had stayed as well. But no one could stop him from being my father's shadow. So, in seconds everyone had their orders of where to search for Igor. Lamar and I would take the back garden. My father and Arkady went to the front of the house. My grandmothers secured the windows and doors with special wards and spells.

My Uncle Andrei and my grandfather had changed into their tigers and would roam the forest to see if they could track Igor down.

Chapter 20

"That bastard escaped once again," I growled. Lamar and I had seen Igor in the garden. The idiot was about to break a window so he could enter the house. Thank God the protection wards and spells had been in place on time. Igor was thrown back, and that had gotten our attention. However, he was on his feet and running before Lamar and I got to him.

We would have gone after him when we heard screaming, and it came from inside the house. "Shit, that's Liam," I said as we started running toward the sliding doors. We rushed into the house, where Lamar and I came to a skidded halt. There, in front of us, stood Eric and Dimitri, and in front of *them* were two dead hyenas.

Liam was covered in blood, as were Eric and Dimitri. "What happened?" I inquired. Felix stood behind Dimitri, and his eyes were too big, and he was too pale. "Tell me later; Felix needs tending because he's in shock." I addressed Eric. "Call Doctor Belinsky; we need him." Dimitri didn't hesitate but immediately reached for his cell phone and hit speed dial.

Liam and Felix were handed a tumbler with whiskey; that had been what the doctor ordered. Both men were alright; thankfully, Felix wasn't in shock.

What about those two? And who are they?" I questioned as I pointed at the two dead hyena shifters. "That's Travis Karr and Boyd Arnett. Boyd did Travis' dirty work," said an unfamiliar voice, making me jump, ready to shift and defend.

"Whoa, easy. I'm David Rendon, and this is Kent Acuna. Your leader Alexei Balashov granted us sanctuary," the one with the red curls and light green eyes said in a calm voice. It was obvious that they didn't want to spook us. I eyed them intently. When I couldn't detect any kind of insincerity, I said, "Welcome. What took you so long? We expected you yesterday, though."

"Titus stopped us. He somehow got wind of us, planning to join the Balshov Streak. So, he captured us and locked us in the cellar," David, the redhead, explained. Felix was trembling. Kent, the one with the dark, short hair, turned to Felix. "Hey, Felix. How are you doing?" he asked, smiling gently at the hyena.

Felix told the two former betas that he was doing alright. "I see that you have met your mate? Congrats," David said, and he was genuinely happy for Felix. "Thank you, David. And, I'm glad that you chose to get away from the clan. You will like it here," Felix said shyly.

Kent's eyes softened when he looked at Felix. "We heard nothing but good things. And seeing you this happy and healthy is a confirmation that the stories are true," he said. Felix blushed. "Yes, it's true. I'm really happy," he replied as he took Dimitri's hand.

"So, where is Alexei?" David asked because he knew that they had to let the leader of the tigers know that they had finally arrived. "My father is checking the premises because Igor was here," I informed the two hyenas. Then, I looked at the two dead ones on the floor and added. "Igor and I guess that Titus is with him as well."

"We know, and we wanted to warn you about the attack, but it took us a while to escape the cellar. I'm sorry," Kent apologized. "No need to apologize," said my father. "Igor escaped," he informed us. "Well, Travis Karr didn't," I said smiling, and it wasn't a pleasant smile.

I stepped aside so my father, Arkady, and Uncle Andrei could see what was lying on the floor. "Well, I guess that we need to call in the cleaning crew," Arkady chuckled. "I already called them; they can arrive any minute now," I informed Arkady. "Where is Milo?" I asked no one in particular. Everyone looked from left to right, but no one answered. My heart was slamming against my ribs. Where was my dog?

The barking came from the back of the house, the garden. "That's Milo," I panted because breathing had become difficult. I stormed out of the room only to stop abruptly. Milo came walking toward the house; he walked slowly because he was dragging a dead hyena with him. "Well, I'll be damned," I whispered. "Well said," Lamar said from behind me.

"I like him," said David. "Me too," Kent agreed wholeheartedly. "Who is he?" I looked from Kent to David. "That's Brent Reyes, also one of Titus' inner circle," said Kent. "Judging by your expression, he wasn't your friend?" I said. Kent and David shook their heads. "No, he was a sadist," said David. "And a coward too," Kent added.

I sighed because Igor had escaped once again. He was the one who knew where my mother was. "We will get him," Lamar promised. I kissed him gently on his soft, full lips. "I know," I replied. My father motioned for David and

Kent to follow him into his study. I would make sure that our cleaning crew got rid of the bodies and the blood.

Dimitri and Eric had taken Felix, Arden, Liam, Ralph, and Justin into the sunroom, away from the massacre. We had an excellent cleaning crew. When they had finished, it was like there had never been a killing. Even the smell was gone.

Still, it didn't change the fact that there had been a small bloodbath in my father's house—a home where we should be safe. I wondered how Travis and Boyd had managed to come into the house. The wards and spells that my two grandmothers had placed should have prevented them from entering the house.

******

I unlocked the front door and stepped inside. I looked around, eyeing the hair washing sinks. The huge mirrors where customers could watch their hair being done. The blow dryers and the trays with scissors and other equipment on them. I inhaled and exhaled, and a feeling of contentment filled me.

The salon was more than successful, and I had the perfect mate; life was good. I left the door unlocked because it was nearly eight in the morning, and soon customers would come in. I had been away from the salon for three days, so now it was adamant that I was present. You can't run a company from a distance, well, not my hair salon anyway. Lamar had tried to talk me into selling the place, but that was not going to happen. The Cutting Edge Hair Salon was my baby, and I wasn't prepared to give that up.

There would come a time when we all would be safe again; it was something that I had to believe. The time would come that we caught Igor and Titus. I knew that once we had them, they would die. Last night, I had dreamed about my mother, and it had been a vivid dream. Now I wondered if it meant something because nothing happened without a reason that much I knew.

I never dreamed or never remembered any of my dreams. Experts say that everyone dreams at least three to four times per night. So, for me to remember the dream about my mother wasn't something to dismiss.

The doorbell jingled, and in walked Jason, my manager, followed by Christine and Jennifer. A moment later, Raoul joined us as well. Now, my staff was complete; it was Saturday, and then it was all hands on deck. We had a lot of appointments, and people who didn't have an appointment would also swing by.

It was seven in the evening when I closed and locked the salon's front door. Milo had stayed with Arkady at his request. I was looking forward to a quiet evening at home with my mate and no one else. Eric and Liam were staying at my father's house. Ralph and Justin had wanted to go home. There was no reason for Igor to come after them, so we had let them go home.

I had almost reached my car when all hell broke loose. I caught the scent too late. They must have used the wind to prevent me from detecting them, the bastards. I was grabbed from behind, but I managed to turn and let my hands grow into claws and slashed his throat. I managed to take out another one as well.

Then, suddenly a really huge tiger appeared, which could only be Igor. Next to him stood a huge hyena; it had to be Titus Karr. Holy hell, they were huge, too big, actually. Why were they so massive? Even my father wasn't that huge. "What the hell?" I growled while I initiated the change. I was in my second form, where I stood on two legs, had a massive head with huge deadly teeth and giant claws.

Why I said the following words, I had no idea. "You want me, then come and get me. But before you do, tell me why you are so hell-bent on seeing me dead?" I had, for a moment, forgotten that shifters in their animal form weren't able to speak.

It was Titus who charged first. I must admit that he was faster than I anticipated. It was why he got the chance to jump me. Before I could react, Titus tried to slash my throat. My reaction was way faster, and that's the only reason that kept him from reaching his goal.

I couldn't prevent that Titus tore my back open, and then he was joined by Igor. Shit, these two weren't only huge, but they also were strong. Christ, how was that possible? Igor had buried his teeth into my left leg, and I howled in pain. It would take a miracle for me not to lose the fight and die.

Even though I was at a loss of how to defend myself, my tiger knew what to do. Not distracted by the pain that Igor inflicted, my tiger knew that he was the more dangerous one. I grabbed Igor by its scruff and threw him away as far as possible. Unfortunately, I couldn't prevent that the bastard tore a piece of flesh from my left leg, which hurt like a bitch.

Igor roared in rage, but I couldn't care less because there still was Titus, and he was relentless. I grabbed or tried to grab Titus by its scruff, but the bastard was fast. So, I missed, then Titus turned and reached for my throat. The damn bastard went for my jugular; well, we couldn't have that. I roared, and then I grabbed Titus by *his* throat. This time he wasn't fast enough. I let my claws sink into his flesh; blood flowed down my arm to the floor.

Titus grabbed my arm; he kept struggling; I must say that it was impressive because a regular shifter would have been dead by now. But not Titus, no, not him. The bastard looked at me, and then he smiled. I squeezed the life out of him, and he smiled? Then I felt a searing pain at the back of my head, which made me see the stars in different freaking colors.

My vision blurred, and for a moment, my world went black. Now I knew why that rat had smiled. He had seen Igor sneaking up from behind so that he could smash my head.

No, not again, I didn't want to be kidnapped, and I certainly didn't want to die, no way. I roared so loud that it even hurt my own ears. I didn't know that I could produce so much volume.

Apparently, I wasn't the only one whose ears hurt by my roar. Titus let go of my arm, and even though I still had him by the throat, he covered his ears. I saw that blood was streaming down the side of his face. That meant only one thing; his eardrums must have ruptured, good.

Igor let go of whatever it was he had hit me with and grabbed his ears as well. I lashed out and managed to slice Igor's face, but I needed to get away, fast. Thank God Igor hadn't been able to hit me for the second time because I might not have survived another blow to the head. Igor and Titus were howling in pain, which gave me the chance to change into my human form, get into my car, and escape.

Chapter 21

"That's it. I'm not letting you go to the salon on your own again," Lamar growled. I didn't have a reply to that because my mate was right. It wasn't safe for me to go anywhere without protection. Well, not anytime soon, anyway. "Baby? Don't fight me on this one," Lamar pleaded. I shook my head. "I wasn't planning to," I softly replied.

The sudden attack had shaken me more than I anticipated. "Mitchell, can you describe how Titus and Igor looked when they attacked you?" my father questioned. "There's not much to say, apart from the fact that they were huge. I mean Titus' hyena has the size of." I looked at my father. "He was even bigger than your tiger," I finally said.

My father frowned, Arkady growled, and Lamar shook his head. My father's tiger was huge. Our animals were larger than normal animals. So, Titus' hyena shouldn't have been larger than a grizzly bear or something. "Titus' hyena was nearly the size as a buffalo. And Igor's tiger was even bigger," I said.

"How on earth did they manage that?" Arkady whispered. "Dark magic," Grandma Anichka said. I looked over my shoulder and saw that both my grandmothers were in the room. "What do you mean by that?" I asked because dark magic sounded serious.

It was Grandma Natalya who spoke. "Our family doesn't associate with warlocks. We know some of them, but we always kept our distance. Igor must have contacted one of the warlocks and asked them for help.”

“Why would they help someone like Igor?” I asked in irritation. Grandma Anichka shrugged. “Money. Revenge, who knows,” she said. “You must know, Kotyonok. Warlocks don’t care for anyone, except for themselves,” Grandma Natalya said.

“If we can manage to know what spell is used, we could reverse it. Then, Igor and Titus’ animals would have their normal size again,” Grandma Natalya said. I pressed my lips together. “Too bad that we don’t know which warlock has helped Igor and Titus. Otherwise, we could make him spill the beans about the dark spell,” I sighed.

“Well, maybe there is a way to reverse the dark spell,” my grandfather said, surprising me. It wasn’t often that he interfered. He was the silent type, but when he spoke, everyone listened. I eyed him in question, and when I didn’t say anything, he continued. “You receive a gift, healing power, right?” I nodded. “What has that to do with?” “Hush,” my grandfather interrupted. “As far as I know, someone who is placed under a dark spell is considered soiled, polluted, if you will,” he paused again and then added, “You could treat the dark spell as a sickness. That way, you can heal Igor and Titus.”

“Why would I heal those two?” I said indignantly because it didn’t make any sense. “Baby, if you heal them, then their animals will be back to their normal size again,” my mate said. “Oh,” I whispered. Lamar chuckled, as did my grandfather. “You’re still learning, Mitchell,” he said, and his smile was gentle.

I had healed Felix, and now I would be able to heal those two psychopaths. "It looks like I got my gift of healing just in time," I remarked. "It seems that way, baby," Lamar agreed.

"You look thoughtful, Mitch. What's on your mind?" Lamar questioned. I looked up, and my mate was correct; there was a lot on my mind. "First," I said, "We need to know who put that thick gray cloud around Felix. It prevented him from getting healthy. Hell, it would have killed him in the end. Then we really need to find Igor because he is the only one who knows where my mother is and Grandpa Borya Vasiliev." I paused because talking about my mother always was emotional for me.

"I want Titus dead because as long as he exists, all our lives are in danger." I paused again, then I added in a whisper. "I want Vera healthy and happy again; I should be able to manage that. Then I need to know who wrote the letter, claiming that Igor killed Elijah on purpose." I heard a deep sigh and saw Dusty looking at me strangely. The man was fighting to keep the tears at bay. Shit, it was hard to see this big, strong warrior so defeated. It only made me more determined to make Vera healthy and happy again.

That thought made me think of Elijah, who had died so violently at such a young age. He was tortured to death, and that must have taken time. A shifter was hard to kill, and they had let him suffer all through the end. Ever since her son's violent death, Vera hadn't eaten and hadn't spoken either. She appeared to be catatonic, and now she was admitted into The Hope Garden Psychiatric Institution for shifters.

I hoped and prayed that they would be able to help her. If not, I would ask Dusty's permission to see if I could help her. After all, I had the gift of healing; it was a very powerful gift at that. So, I hoped that I would be able to help her if anything else failed.

"By now, Titus must know that his younger brother didn't make it. That Travis and Boyd both are dead." I eyed David and Kent, the two hyenas who had joined us; I said, "How fond is Titus of his baby brother?" David raised one eyebrow, and Kent looked thoughtful. It was David who finally spoke. "It might sound strange what I'm about to tell you. Titus adored Travis; it was almost sickening; he basically worshipped him. I mean, I love my family, but I don't worship them; that would be sick."

I nodded in agreement because the man was right. I loved my father, but I didn't worship him. I did, however, worship my mate. "Why do you ask?" Kent questioned. "I hope that the knowledge of Travis being killed by one of the tigers, and or wolves, will drive him over the edge. He will lose what little common sense he has and will attack without thinking things through," I was thinking out loud now.

"Maybe we are lucky, and Igor will try and stop him," Lamar added. "That would be the icing on the cake," I said, grinning.

I needed some fresh air, so I crossed the room to the sliding doors and stepped onto the back deck. It was where my father found me a moment later. "Is everything alright?" "Yes, I'm fine. It's just, well, I want Igor and Titus dead. I hate to see Vera in such a fragile state. The woman still doesn't speak. At least Doctor Krause managed to get Vera to eat," I sighed.

"As long as Igor and Titus are roaming the streets, no one is safe. It dictates our lives, and I've had enough. It's time that we end it, once and for all," I softly added. In fact, I was tired of looking over my shoulder and tensing up whenever I heard an unfamiliar sound. I wanted to go to the salon every day. In short, I wanted my life back, and I would get it back. That was a promise to myself.

I was part wizard, after all, and that had to count for something. Furthermore, Grandma Natalya was a very powerful witch, even though she, just like me, only was part witch. My other grandmother Anichka brewed the best potions. Also, she could draw powerful wards, which had protected us more than once.

Thank God I had taken some blood samples before the cleaning crew had arrived. I could use it for scrying to find Titus. Well, he was a shifter, but still, I would try because one never knew. "Mitchell? Mitchell?" I shook my head and stared in confusion at my father. "I heard you the first time, dad," I said. "No, son. I called your name more than ten times. You didn't react," my father said.

"What's going on?" a worried-looking Lamar asked. "I'm alright, really. I think I spaced out, but I'm fine," I answered truthfully. "I need to talk to my grandmothers," I said as I jumped up and rushed inside. I heard my father and Lamar follow me into the living room.

I found both women in the kitchen; they were busy with dessert. "I need to." "We know what you need, Kotyonok," Grandma Natalya said. I smiled, I didn't have any idea how she did it, but she seemed to know the things I wanted to do before I did.

"I'll wait until you finish making dessert," I said. Grandma Anichka laughed. "Oh, boy. We are working on a potion so you can start scrying for Titus Karr," she informed me. I eyed both women intently, then I softly said, "No dessert? You really are scary, sometimes." They laughed.

Chapter 22

"Come here, baby," Lamar pulled me close; he whispered, "Titus won't escape us, nor will the others," I nodded. "Now, let me make love to you," Lamar whispered as his hand slid into my sweatpants. I moaned when Lamar cupped my balls and gently started massaging them. "Yes, that feels good, oh yes," I panted.

Lamar's touch was electrifying yet gentle and reassuring. I loved it when he touched me like that. It made me feel like I was the most precious person in his life, which, of course, I was. But knowing it, or actually feeling it, were two very different things. Lamar always made me feel good, no matter what he did, what he said, or how he acted. I always came first. It was the same between the sheets; he always ensured that I was thoroughly loved. I, of course, felt the same. To me, Lamar was the most important person in my life.

Lamar's hand slid out of my sweatpants and pulled them down. I moved my legs to get rid of the sweats, so I could spread my legs. Lamar lazily stroked my inner thigh, which made me shiver with need. I wanted my mate to fuck me into oblivion, but I knew that it wouldn't happen. Not so soon, anyway. Lamar would take his time worshipping my body, as he always did.

Fingers trailed slowly from my inner thigh toward my abdomen and then my nipples. I moaned because I knew what was coming next, and I wasn't disappointed. Lamar's wet tongue followed his fingers; he licked and nibbled his way up to my nipples. Then he started sucking them, and I lost it when he playfully bit the hard nubs.

My cock went even stiffer, and then hot creamy seed splashed between us. Lamar lifted his head and smiled. "So eager. I love that you react to me like that," he whispered. I couldn't reply because I still was gasping for air after coming so hard.

Lamar sucked my earlobe, licked my neck, and said, "Spread your legs for me, baby." I did without hesitation. My cock still was hard even though I had already ejaculated once. Lamar slid down toward my erection, kept looking in my eyes as his lips closed around my needy cock. "Oh, yes yes," I kept chanting because my mate's mouth and tongue were heavenly. Lamar sucked and let his tongue swirl around my stiff shaft.

Lamar began to suck harder and harder. He grabbed my hips to keep me from bucking too hard. One time I had bucked so violently that I had thrown Lamar off the bed. Afterward, we had laughed so loud. Lamar was a man with a mission, and that mission was making me a very happy mate.

While sucking my rock-hard erection, Lamar gently stroked my inner thighs again. He knew that I loved it and that it would make me want more. I felt my balls tighten and protested when suddenly, he stopped sucking and stroking.

Lamar crept up until we were face to face, kissed me, and drove two fingers into me. It felt like I was on fire. I gasped for air, Lamar chuckled. He pushed in hard every time because he knew that, as a shifter, I could take it. I lifted my hips in anticipation. It always felt so good to have his fingers inside me. It was almost as good as Lamar's massive erection.

My mate managed to playfully lick my cock while his fingers brought me heavenly pleasure. This was one of those love-making sessions where it was all about me. It was not because I wanted it, but because my mate had decided it.

I was staring at Lamar because I was mesmerized whenever he made love to me. The man was a powerful alpha, and to others, he was the strong silent type. But, he was the perfect mate for me because he was loving, kind, sensitive, protective.

Lamar pulled his fingers out of me, wrapped his hand around his massive erection, positioned it, and then he pushed in, hard. I gasped because Lamar wasn't careful; he didn't stop until he was entirely inside me. "Move, babe. Please move," I begged like I always did when he didn't move fast enough, in my opinion.

Lamar smiled, pulled out slowly, and then he slammed into me again, using full force. I started moving my hips, and a moment later, we moved in perfect unison. This was the best moment because that way, Lamar could penetrate me even deeper.

"Oh baby, that's it, my love. You're mine, all mine. I can do with you what I want," Lamar panted as he slowly was losing his rhythm. I knew that he was close, just as I was.

"I'm yours to do with as you please, babe. I'm all yours, always. Now, let me have it, big guy," I panted and growled at the same time. Lamar always drove me crazy. I knew that I could drive him over the edge by telling him that I was his, for always. It didn't take long before Lamar went rigid and nearly crushed my hips when he came.

Lamar's cock swelled even more; when he came, I could feel it, literally feel it getting bigger. Feeling Lamar's shaft grow drove me over the edge. I grabbed Lamar's hair, our gazes locked, then I came for the second time. All the time, we kept looking into each other's eyes. I thought that I would lose my mind, it was always like this, with my mate.

I turned on my back, trying to catch my breath; Lamar did the same. For a moment, neither said a word. The house was quiet, which was good. But, with so many people staying at the mansion, it became crowded sometimes. We couldn't go back to our home because it was too dangerous. The pack would protect us, but we didn't want to risk any of their lives. And since our pack and the Balashov Streak had become allies, it was better to stick together.

I must admit that the wolves and the tigers cooperated really well together. Maybe it was because I was mated to the alpha of the McLaughlin Pack. Anyway, I was glad that everyone worked together so well. It would keep us safe, or as safe as it could be.

"Are you alright," Lamar asked when he saw my expression. I shook my head because, no, I wasn't okay. Lamar wrapped me in his arms and held me tightly. "You survived, and you will be okay," Lamar soothed as he kissed the top of my head. I sighed, I felt safe right now, but I knew that danger was around the corner.

Igor was a dangerous man, and he was a force to be reckoned with. I had underestimated him once; it wouldn't happen again. "Don't let him into your head, baby. It won't do you any good," Lamar softly said. "I know, but." "No, baby. You will be fine. You're one of the strongest shifters I know. Keep that in mind, always," Lamar insisted.

Then, Lamar went into the bathroom and returned with a warm, wet washcloth. I was too tired to shower, and Lamar knew me so well. He cleaned me, and I didn't even remember closing my eyes.

Chapter 23

"I want to talk to him," I said. Dusty frowned. "You would have to ask Doctor Krause if that's possible," he answered solemnly. I decided to call the doctor to get permission to talk to the man who insisted that he knew Igor and Titus' whereabouts.

Dusty had visited his mate, Vera, at The Hope Garden Psychiatric Institution, where she was admitted after she refused to eat and talk. It was where he had met Ronan, a hawk shifter. The man had insisted that he wanted to talk to me, and only me.

"Are you sure that it's wise to go to the institution? I mean, I could be a trap," Lamar softly said. I could tell that the man was worried, and he had every right to be. "If things go south, then you'll be there," I said as I cuddled up to my mate. Lamar smiled; he softly said, "I'm glad that you don't resist my protection anymore."

Igor and Titus, attacking me in their massive shapes, had been a close call, too close, which could have cost me my life. But, even though I was stubborn, at times, I wasn't stupid or too proud to accept my mate's protection. "I feel safe knowing that you're near to step in should it become necessary I told Lamar. My mate smiled in relief.

"It looks nice enough," I said. We were standing in front of the building of the mental institution for shifters. Somewhere inside was Vera, and I hoped and prayed that they would be able to help her. However, now it was about the hawk shifter. Dusty hadn't known his name. The hawk hadn't told him, which told me how scared the man was to be discovered. Apparently, the hawk had been nearly killed by Igor and Titus. He had been able to escape, but barely.

Lamar insisted on accompanying me inside the building. We walked toward the desk, where I told the woman that I had an appointment with Doctor Krause. Lamar sniffed the air and wasn't subtle about it either; there was no need because this was shifter territory.

A moment later, a very handsome man came toward us, a serious expression on his face. "Hello, I'm Doctor Krause," he said as he held out his hand in greeting. I took the offered hand, and we shook. Then Lamar did the same. Doctor Krause looked from me to Lamar, he said in an apologetic tone. "I can only give Mitchell permission to see the hawk."

I frowned. "You say hawk? You didn't say the man's name; why is that?" I questioned because it was odd. "I know that it must sound odd, but it was at the hawk's request. It tells us how scared he is," the doctor explained.

"I see." "So, I hope that you take that into consideration when you talk to him," Doctor Krause said. "I will," I promised. "Alright, I'll take you to him then," the doctor said. Then he eyed Lamar. "I guess that you want to wait here, to make sure that your mate stays safe?" "Yes, absolutely," Lamar said. "Alright then, Karen will show you to the waiting room. You are allowed to use your phone to call your mate if you feel the need. Although, I recommend that you don't. It could disturb his interview with the hawk," the doctor explained. "I'll be alright," I said as I kissed Lamar and then followed the doctor.

Dusty had filled me in about Vera's condition. She still didn't talk, but she had eaten a bit. The doctor stopped and softly knocked on the door to our right. He opened the door and peeked inside. "Mitchell is here to see you," the doctor said as he opened the door a bit further and motioned for me to enter the room.

"Hi," I softly said as I slowly stepped into the room. He smiled, and to my astonishment, said, "You don't need to be so careful. I trust you. If I didn't, I wouldn't have sent for you." I smiled. "That makes sense," I replied. "Is it alright if I sit down?" "Sure." So I took the chair and placed it opposite the hawk.

"As you know, I'm Mitchell. Care to tell me your name?" I started carefully. "Sure, but only if you promise me not to tell anyone else. If Igor finds out where I am," the hawk paused. I said, "Igor and Titus attacked me the previous night. I escaped, but barely. Did you know that their animals are massive?"

The hawk looked surprised. "No, I did not know. What exactly do you mean when you say massive," the hawk asked. I noticed that the hawk seemed comfortable in my presence, which was good. "However, the hawk still hadn't told me his name. Then, as if reading my thoughts, the hawk said, "My name is Ronan. Ronan Haas. As you know, I'm a hawk shifter."

"Hi, Ronan Haas. It's nice to meet you," I said as I held out my hand. To my joy, Ronan took my offered hand, and we shook. Ronan eyed me intently, then he said in a barely audible voice, "Did you get my letter?" It took me a few seconds, but then it hit me, oh hell. "Tell me what you wrote, please. It's not that I don't trust you, but."

Alright, I didn't trust him because I didn't know the guy. But, he seemed sincere enough; I couldn't detect any lie.

"I wrote to you about Igor, torturing Elijah," Ronan whispered as tears filled his eyes. "Every time I close my eyes, I see him, lying there, and." I stood, sat beside Ronan on the edge of the bed, and put my arm around his shoulder. Ronan shook. "It's alright, let it out. I'm here and will be for as long as you need me," I promised. "Do you mean it?" "Yes, I never say things I don't mean," I assured Ronan. It took a long time before Ronan had calmed down enough to talk to me.

"Even though you haven't been a shifter that long, you have built quite a reputation. You are fair, kind and always helping the ones who are in need," Ronan said. I raised my eyebrows because I didn't know I had a reputation. "You didn't know?" Ronan said. I shook my head. "No," I replied. "Oh, and many bad guys are scared to death of you," Ronan chuckled.

I frowned because this was news to me. So the bad guys were afraid of me? "Well, that's good, I guess," I replied. Then I asked Ronan if he was able to go on sharing his information about Elijah. I knew that it must be hell for the poor hawk shifter. It was there, in his eyes, the man lived in his personal hell. I really wanted to pull him out of the bad place he was in, but now was not the time.

Ronan's voice trembled when he started to explain. "I was there when they captured poor Elijah. They made me watch as they tortured him." Ronan paused and turned his head away from me. I was at a loss of what to do. The man was traumatized, so much was clear. But, the fact was that I didn't have any experience with traumatized shifters. So, I waited until Ronan turned toward me again.

Ronan grabbed his head, and his shoulders shook; the shifter was crying. "Every time I close my eyes, I not only see his bloody and mutilated body, but I hear him scream in pain," Ronan whispered. "I can't go on living like this; it has to stop." Again, I felt rage like I seldom had felt.

It wasn't only that they had kidnapped my mother, and probably Grandfather Borya Vasiliev. No, they had left a trail of destruction, so many lives had been affected. Igor, Titus, and this Doyle had caused so much damage, and it was time to put an end to it, once and for all. We needed to find and eliminate those monsters. But not before I had my answers, and I would get my answers, one way or another. If I had to torture them, I would do so because these weren't humans or shifters. No, they were monsters, and I would treat them accordingly.

"I saw that Vera Reed was admitted. Do you know how she's doing? They won't tell me, and they won't let anyone near her," Ronan said. I shook my head because I had been lost in my thoughts. I knew that the doctor had ordered to keep Vera apart from the rest of the patients. It was at my mate and Dusty's request because they were afraid she wouldn't be safe if word spread that she was committed.

I decided that it was safe to inform Ronan about Vera's situation; after all, the man had witnessed the torture and death of Elijah, her son. It was Ronan who had taken the pictures to prove that he hadn't been lying. I couldn't even begin to imagine how difficult that must have been. It wasn't only that the hawk shifter had been beaten to an inch of his life. No, he had been badly damaged, psychologically.

There was a soft knock, and the doctor peeked inside. "Just a few more minutes because it's time for your therapy, Ronan," Doctor Krause said. Ronan nodded. I was pleased that he had addressed Ronan instead of me. The doctor closed the door again, and Ronan and I stared at each other. "You have our protection, and if they release you, then you will have a place at the home I share with my mate, Lamar McLaughlin," I promised Ronan.

I had seen the question and the uncertainty in the hawk shifter's eyes. The man had nowhere to go after his release. Plus, he would be in danger because Igor and especially Doyle, the leader of the hawks, would want his head on a stick. There were only two places where Ronan would be safe, my home and my father's estate.

"Don't you need to talk to your mate before you open your home to me?" Ronan was baffled. I smiled. "No, I don't because Lamar will understand," I assured my new friend. "Thank you," Ronan whispered.

I stood and pulled Ronan into a firm hug, then I gently pushed him at arm's length and said, "I need to go now because you have therapy, and I have things to do. But I'll be back tomorrow. You have my word."

Chapter 24

"I urge you not to try and heal Vera," Grandma Anichka said solemnly. We were having breakfast when I had brought up the subject of healing Vera and Ronan. "Why not? She's suffering every freaking day," I said because I didn't understand. Why was Grandma Anichka so dead set against me healing Vera Reed? The woman had suffered a tremendous loss, and she had the right to be happy again. "Your grandmother is right, Kotyonok." I frowned because what the hell? "Why?" I said, and I knew I sounded slightly irritated, but I couldn't help it.

"You explain it to him, Anichka," Grandma Natalya said. My grandmother gently smiled; she softly said, "Vera Reed is too damaged to be healed right now. She still has a lot to process. If her mind doesn't get the time to do so, then you would do more harm than good. Vera will need months, maybe years even."

Shit, I hadn't thought of that. "Don't beat yourself up about that. They have many years of experience on you, Mitchell," my father chuckled. Well, that was true. "Are you calling us old?" Grandma Natalya scoffed good naturally. "No, of course not. I wouldn't dare," my father laughed as he left the room. "Well, we could put him under a spell," Grandma Anichka chuckled. Both women found it very funny because they started laughing.

Then both women looked serious again; Grandma Natalya said, "Do you have what we need to scry for Igor?" I could tell that both women would gladly cut off Igor's balls when we got our hands on him. Yes, it wasn't a matter of if, but when, because we would capture him, of that I was sure. "I do," I said as I left to get some of Igor's flesh that I ripped off his face when he and Titus had attacked me in front of the salon.

I hadn't even known that I had torn a piece of flesh from Igor's massive tiger until I had seen it in my car, lying on the floor. I had wanted to throw it away, but Grandma Anichka had told me to keep it. I had bought a special freezer for the piece of flesh because the thought of having it between my food had made my stomach turn.

"Well, Anichka, we need a spell. Would you do the honors?" Grandma Natalya said. "Of course, dear,' Grandma Anichka replied as she went into the sunroom to start writing a spell. Igor wasn't a wizard, so there was more needed than only a piece of his flesh. Grandma Natalya and I would make a potion using part of Igor's flesh. Then, with the spell and the rest of Igor's flesh and combined powers, we should be able to summon the bastard. Igor was family, which made it possible to scry for the shifter.

It turned out that Grandma Anichka needed more time to come up with a spell powerful enough to support the potion. It gave me the time to visit Ronan in the mental facility. I had spoken to Lamar and my father about healing Ronan and then bringing him home. Both had thought it an excellent idea, which had pleased me very much.

When I was at The Hope Garden Psychiatric Institution, I had been told that Vera's condition hadn't changed. Doctor Krause had confirmed what my grandmothers had warned me about. Vera was significantly mentally damaged. And according to the doctor, it would take years for her to come to terms with her son's death.

There even was the chance that she wouldn't recover at all. A patient only could recover if the treatment went well. Right now, Vera didn't want to live anymore. So the doctors had to work on that first before they could start with the actual treatment.

The visitors who came to see a patient had to wait outside in the garden or the family room. I had permission to visit Ronan in his room. I softly knocked. "Come in, Mitchell," Ronan sounded better than yesterday. "Hey. How are you? How did you sleep?" I asked as we hugged. "Don't ask," Ronan replied as we sat down.

"I want to talk to you about something. But, if you don't like the idea, you need to tell me honestly. I'm not forcing you into anything," I said. Ronan frowned, but then he said, "Alright. I'm listening."

"I don't know if you are aware of the fact that I'm more than just a shifter," I began carefully. Ronan looked confused, so I assumed he didn't know I had a second form or was part wizard. I explained what I was and that recently, I had received the gift of healing. "Would you be able to heal me? Well, at least to give me back my peace of mind. I need to be able to close my eyes without." Ronan paused as tears filled his eyes.

"I can try," I said because I didn't know how it would turn out. "It's all very new to me, and I don't have much experience yet," I said. I was as honest as I could be because Ronan had to make a tough decision. After all, he didn't know me. To him, I still was a stranger. Ronan only knew me by reputation. "Do it," he said. "Are you sure?" "Yep, I am. I somehow trust you," he said. I smiled because to hear those words was a huge compliment. To me, it was important that people who I was about to help trusted me. Ronan was sincere.

"Alright, but I need you to come with me to my father's estate," I said carefully. I needed him in my father's house because my grandmothers were there as well. They lived on the estate. Plus, I was most powerful. It was so strange because I loved the house that Lamar and I had built. Still, I felt more at home at my father's estate. Well, maybe it was because most of my family lived there as well.

"Let's do this. I want to feel normal again," Ronan said. Even though Ronan was an emotional mess, him, I could help. And damn, I would help him get his life back. So, Ronan was on board; now, I had to convince Doctor Krause to release Ronan into my care. As if reading my thoughts or sensing my worries, Ronan said, "They can't keep me here against my will. It's not how they operate."

It turned out that Doctor Krause thought it was good for Ronan to come and live with Lamar and me for a while. He knew how protective the Balashov Streak and the McLaughlin Pack were. Doctor Krause also told Ronan that he would be there for him if he needed to talk. So, after that was settled, I helped Ronan pack his things. I had, however, called Lamar to tell him that Ronan had agreed to come home with me. So, when we stepped outside, Lamar was already waiting. With him were three enforcers and three soldiers of my father's streak.

It was because I knew how dangerous Igor, Titus, and Doyle were. That I couldn't guarantee to keep Ronan safe should they decide to attack. Even though it was broad daylight, I knew that it wouldn't stop them from attacking me. Yes, that's how deranged they were.

"Hey, baby," Lamar greeted before he kissed me. "Hey," I said, slightly out of breath. Lamar's kisses did that to me. The rest greeted Ronan and me. "Let's get out of here," I said. Everyone got into their car, and then we drove to my father's estate.

"Hello, you must be Ronan," Grandma Natalya said as she held out her hand. Ronan smiled tentatively as he took the offered hand. "Sit sit," Grandma Natalya urged. Then she put food on the table; Ronan watched with interest when more and more food was placed on the table. "We have many mouths to feed," Grandma Natalya smiled.

Soon everyone sat at the table having lunch; only Ronan wasn't eating. He drank his water, but that was all. "Ronan, you need to eat," Grandma Anichka urged. Ronan told her that he wasn't hungry, but grandma Anichka insisted; she said, "No, really, Ronan. You need to eat because before Mitchell can help you, you need to get your strength back. If your body is weak because you're refusing to eat, he can't heal you." "I can't?" "No, you can't," Grandma Anichka said. Well, I would have to ask her later what she meant because I was getting confused.

When I received the gift of healing, I thought that I could heal everyone; apparently, I had been wrong. According to Grandma Anichka, Vera Reed's mental state had to improve before I could start healing her. And even then, I couldn't heal her completely; she would need several sessions. And Ronan was physically too weak to be healed. Grandma Anichka had explained that it would cost Ronan's body a tremendous amount of energy to heal. That's why Ronan had to eat and drink, to regain his strength again.

I eyed Ronan. "My grandmother knows about these things. And I trust her judgment. So, at least try and eat something," I urged. It looked like Ronan would refuse, but then he took a sandwich and slowly took a small bite. I nodded my approval. I had the feeling that Ronan suffered from survivor's guilt. Elijah was dead; he was not. Grandma Anichka stood and strode out of the room. She motioned for me to follow. I excused myself, and my father and Lamar would keep Ronan company.

Arkady, who had joined us for lunch, hadn't said one word. But I could tell that he was furious. Well, furious wasn't the right word; the man was enraged. My father had told me that Arkady had never liked Igor, and he had never trusted the man either. Even though Arkady was proven correct, the man had never said a word about how right he had been all those years. It told me a lot about Arkady; he had integrity and honor.

"What is it that you want to talk about?" I said when we were outside. Apparently, we would take a walk through the garden, which was fine by me. I loved being outdoors, even it was so much a stroll through the beautiful garden.

"There's a lot that you don't know, especially about your gift to heal," she began. When I didn't say anything, she continued. "Your ability to heal is very strong, very powerful. It certainly is a reason to be extra cautious if you heal someone. Take Ronan; his body is too weak to accept your healing. If you healed him today, you probably would kill him. If Ronan regains his strength, and you throw all your healing power at once at him, it probably would kill him too," Grandma Anichka paused, and her expression was grim.

"I didn't have any idea how powerful you really are, Mitchell. Grandma Natalya and I will need to teach you how to manage your power." "I don't understand. Well, I do, but." "You still are learning to control your tiger, Kotyonok. Now you need to manage your healing power as well." It was Grandma Natalya who had interrupted me. "Shush," she said when I opened my mouth to protest. I closed my mouth again and eyed her.

Grandma Natalya nodded, then smiled. "Let me finish before you start your protest," she softly said. I nodded, Grandma Natalya continued. "You must know that everything is connected. It means that your healing power is also connected to your tiger. If you lost control over your tiger, you also would lose control over your healing power."

"I don't understand. Why should my tiger get the upper hand if I heal someone?" I asked in confusion. I knew that there were many things I still had to learn in my life as a shifter. I also knew that my tiger gained the upper hand every now and then. It happened less and less, but it still wasn't good. Everyone I knew had perfect control over their animals, except for me.

"What would happen when you are working on Ronan, healing the man, and your tiger would sense danger?" Grandma Natalya said. I opened my mouth to answer, but I didn't know what to say. I simply didn't have an answer. Because, yes, what would I do?

Both grandmothers smiled when they saw that the lights went on. "You're right. It would be a catastrophe for sure." But then, it dawned that it would be more than that. "If I can't control my tiger, I could kill Ronan in the process," I whispered. Both women nodded.

Chapter 25

"Breathe in, breathe out, slowly," whispered Grandma Anichka. "You need to relax more, honey. You're still too tense," she added. I opened my eyes because this was so much harder than I anticipated. Yoga and meditation, well, it wasn't so easy as it looked. "I'm sorry, but I can't seem to concentrate, grandma," I apologized. I knew that it was of utmost importance that I learned to control my emotions so I would be able to keep my tiger in check.

"You'll learn, Kotyonok," Grandma Natalya softly said. Well, for now, it didn't look like I would. "Really, you will learn. Your biggest problem is concentration. It's something we have to work on first before we teach you how to meditate," said Grandma Anichka. I sighed.

My father came into the sunroom. "How are things going?" he questioned, smiling. "Not so good," I scowled. My father laughed; he said, "What did you expect? It's not that you learn to meditate in an hour; it takes weeks, months even."

I didn't like that one bit because I didn't have the time. Hell, Ronan didn't have that time; the man was suffering every single day. "Well, I don't have weeks or months even. Ronan needs to be healed as soon as possible," I said. My father nodded, looked at his mother, my Grandmother Natalya, and nodded. She nodded back in return, I frowned.

Before I could ask what that was all about, Grandma Natalya said, "Your Grandmother Anichka and I could brew a potion that would subdue your tiger." When I opened my mouth to say no way, she softly added, "Think before you answer, Kotyonok."

So, I thought about that. On the one hand, it would allow me to help Ronan right away. But, on the other, when my tiger was subdued, it wouldn't be able to sense danger. Let alone help in case of an attack.

"It will only be for a few hours. Plus, everyone will be here, just in case. I believe that combined; we should be able to defend ourselves and keep you and Ronan safe," my father said. He sounded so serious; I guess that was what made me consent. My father, Lamar, and the rest would keep us safe, of that I was sure. And Grandma Natalya was a powerful witch, even though she was only part witch.

"Alright, but I need to know what exactly the potion does to my tiger," the moment I asked the question, my animal began to growl, shit. "What is it, son?" my father asked; yes, the man was perceptive. "My tiger," that was all I was able to say before I shifted, against my will, I might add. Then, my tiger took off. This was so not what I wanted or needed right now. I needed my tiger to be calm and submissive and not behave like a rogue.

"FREEZE, STOP," I yelled as loud as I could because it was the only thing I could think of. I hoped to shock my tiger so much that it would freeze. And lo and behold, the animal did stop. I inhaled and exhaled, then concentrated on shifting back into my human form. Lamar came toward me and handed me a pair of sweats.

"What happened just now?" he asked. "That's what I like to know too," said my father, who had followed

Lamar. "Well, my tiger didn't like the idea of being subdued, so it took control and bolted," I explained. "How did you make it stop and be able to shift back?" my father asked. "Didn't you hear me scream?" I said. Lamar and my father shook their heads simultaneously.

I frowned because I had been screaming very loud. "I yelled for it to freeze. I screamed as loud as I could, and my tiger stopped running. Didn't you hear me yelling? I believe that I was very loud." "No, I didn't," Lamar replied. "I didn't hear you either," my father said.

"That's odd because I know for sure that I yelled very loud. Hell, they must have heard me at the mansion," I said. "Anyway, let's go inside," Lamar said as he held out his hand. I took the offered hand, and the three of us walked toward the house.

"This could mean that you gained control over your tiger," Grandma Anichka said. "That would be good because then we don't need to subdue it," I said. The moment the words left my mouth, my tiger purred in contentment. That was when I knew that he wouldn't stir trouble. I mentally thanked it, then I said, "My tiger won't be a problem. So, we don't need to subdue it."

"Does anyone know where Ronan is? I want to start healing him as soon as possible." "I'm right here," said a soft voice. I turned and was shocked to see the sunken eyes and dark circles under the hawk's eyes. Shit, I knew that I couldn't wait any longer. "When do we start?" Ronan asked while he eyed me expectantly. "Whenever you're ready, Ronan," I replied.

Ronan chose the sunroom where I would start healing him. My grandmothers had warned me not to be too aggressive and take my time. They told me that it would take more than one session before Ronan even came close to being healed. It was because the man was severely damaged. It was the same reason that I couldn't start healing Vera Reed. She was even more damaged, and her mind needed time to recuperate. It probably would have driven her mad if I had started healing her.

I looked at both my grandmothers. "I need your help because I need complete silence so I can entirely focus on Ronan. Can you do that?" I asked. I hoped that both women would be so powerful to seal the room. They eyed each other. I suspected that they were silently talking to each other and that it wasn't the first time.

"Of course we can, Kotyonok," Grandma Natalya chuckled. *Baby, have you any idea how powerful your grandmothers are when they combine their powers?* To feel Lamar's voice flow through my mind made me almost jump. I slowly was getting used to hearing him in my head. In the beginning, Lamar had been cautious when using our mind link. I smiled, and my grandmother looked from Lamar to me and back to Lamar again. It was a knowing look; damn, they knew that Lamar had used our mind link.

"We feel it when you communicate via your mind link," said Grandma Anichka. "But we don't know what you're saying. So, no worries," Grandma Natalya chuckled. I blushed because Lamar and I had more than once shared our erotic thoughts via our mind link.

"We need about an hour to seal the sunroom," said Grandma Anichka. I thanked her and Grandma Natalya, then guided Ronan out of the room. During the hour that we needed to wait, I would explain to Ronan what I was capable of. Ronan needed to know what to expect because to start the healing process, I needed him completely relaxed. The hawk shifter had to trust me entirely too. He needed to open up and let me look into his soul. Otherwise, I wouldn't be able to help him. The soul was something sacred, something so intimate that it had to be handled carefully and with the utmost respect.

We sat on the back deck opposite each other; Ronan eyed me with curiosity. "Alright, I need to ask you some things, and you must answer honestly. If you're not sincere, then I won't be able to help you," I said. Ronan didn't hesitate; he said, "Ask away."

"I will explain what to expect when I start the healing process." When Ronan nodded but stayed silent, I went on. "I start by searching your mind for intruders. Sometimes a witch or wizard can place a spell, which can make you sick. We had that problem with Felix. He didn't get better, and we didn't know why. It turned out that a thick gray kind of mist surrounded him. It rejected everything that could heal him."

"Did you get rid of it? The gray mist, I mean?" Ronan quietly asked. I nodded, "But it took a lot of energy. He's fine now," I said. "That's good. I know and like Felix. For a hyena, he's very nice. Too nice, I would say. That's why Titus and Travis always tortured him," Ronan said solemnly. My curiosity was aroused. "What do you mean by that's why they always tortured him?" I questioned.

Ronan sighed. "They wanted him to, well, man up. Their words, not mine," he added hastily. "I still don't understand." And I didn't because by torturing someone, you only damaged that person. "They had that stupid idea that if they hurt Felix enough, he would snap and turn into a psychopath. They wanted him to be as disturbed as they were themselves." Ronan smiled when he said, "They never succeeded. Felix still is sweet and kind." "Yeah, he is," I replied.

"So, back to you again, Ronan. I will begin by searching your body, mind, and soul for anything that doesn't belong there. That will take a while, and when I don't find anything out of the ordinary, I will continue the healing. I will penetrate your mind. I need you to open up completely, no hesitation. I have to warn you, though, if you open up completely, it means that you can't hide anything from me. I will know all your secrets and desires." I was eyeing Ronan intently.

"Do you know Felix's secrets and desires too?" Ronan carefully asked. I nodded. "Yes, I do, and I will take them with me into my grave, as I will your secrets and desires," I promised. "Then let's do this because I need my sanity intact," Ronan whispered. We talked a bit more until Lamar came onto the deck and let us know that my two grandmothers had finished sealing the sunroom.

"Choose a seat where you feel most comfortable," I said, And Ronan chose the chair in the further's corner away from the windows. I knelt in front of him. "Close your eyes and relax. All you need to do is open up to me, and I'll do the rest." Ronan closed his eyes, and his shoulders slumped a bit, a sign that he was relaxed.

"You will feel me penetrate your mind. Stay relaxed, and welcome me. Embrace my presence," I whispered soothingly. To my joy, Ronan did welcome me into his mind. I had no trouble moving around. I knew I had to tread carefully as not to damage his brain. I couldn't find anything wrong with Ronan's brain, so I searched his body. That was alright, too; now it was time for the trickiest part of my journey into Ronan's mind, body, and soul. I carefully slowly penetrated Ronan's soul. I saw his hawk and was in awe of its beauty. The bird was something else; I'll say that.

Then something else caught my attention, and I sighed because this wasn't what I had hoped for. I can't describe the soul; it's a feeling, kind of. Maybe a transparent cloud, if you will. There, on the edge of Ronan's soul, was a dark spot. It was tiny, but I had seen it. This was so not good. The shifter had a tainted soul? How was that possible? Ronan was a good person, kind, and always helped those who needed it.

I tried to touch the dark spot, but that turned out to be a bad idea. The moment I touched the dark, I was thrown out. My eyes flew open, as did Ronan's. "What the hell was that?" he whispered. I looked at him. Thank God he wasn't hurt.

Chapter 26

"Does that make me a bad person? Because I'm not a bad guy, honestly, I'm not," Ronan kept repeating. "No, it doesn't make you a bad person, Ronan," I soothed. "I believe that someone cast a spell and that way tainted your soul," I tried to explain as best as I could.

"Why would someone do such a thing?" Arden said. The hyena had entered the room quietly as he always did. Felix stood next to him, Dimitri at his side. "I believe that Doyle thought that if Ronan's soul were tainted, he would go bad. However, it's not that simple. It never is," Grandma Anichka explained. I had to admit; the woman had excellent knowledge.

Ronan sighed in relief. "You need to rest, and we will figure out how to cleanse your soul," Grandma Natalya softly said. Ronan went upstairs, followed by Felix and Arden. Lamar's phone rang, and he frowned as he answered the call. A few moments later, he cursed. "The mental hospital is under attack, goddammit." No one questioned my mate, but everyone jumped into action.

Eric Stone, the beta of the McLaughlin Pack, trackers Scott and Simon, and Dimitri, would stay at the estate to guard and defend Liam, Felix, Arden, and Ronan.

We arrived at the clinic in record time, and everyone jumped out of their cars and spread out. Lamar, my father, and I rushed through the front door, where the fighting was in full swing. Hyenas, tigers, and wolves were fighting the staff and guards. "We need to get to Vera's room," I yelled

because I had a feeling that the clinic was under attack
because they wanted her. Goddamn, hadn't they hurt the
Reed family enough? And who was so determined to
destroy the Reeds? I would look into that later, after the
fight.

I knew where Vera's room was, and when we ran into
the hall, we saw Dusty fighting three hyenas who tried to
pass him to get to Vera. I cursed again, and then I initiated
the change. Not my second form but my regular one, and
then I charged forward.

I pulled one hyena off dusty's back; it seemed that
Dusty hadn't even noticed that he had a hyena clawing his
back. I clammed my teeth around its throat and shook. Its
eyes went wide with fear. He shook his head as if saying
no. Then, I bit down hard, and the damn beast stopped
moving. And no, I didn't feel pity for those beasts. Three
of them had been fighting Dusty simultaneously, cowards.

I had expected Vera to scream or try to help her mate,
but no such luck. Instead, she was sitting on the bed,
staring into nothing. My father and Lamar took care of the
two other hyenas. Then Dusty looked up, "Titus," he
growled, and then he was gone, using shifter speed.

Shit, this wasn't good. I turned and ran after Dusty
because Titus wouldn't be alone. He had a right to fight
and kill the bastard. I would see to it that no one interfered.
It was bloody when Dusty roared and attacked a surprised
Titus. Damn, that bastard had thought that the three hyenas
would have killed Dusty? Had Titus ordered the kill?

Dusty went for Titus' throat but missed. Titus managed
to slash Dusty's side, and ribs became visible. Dusty roared
in rage. It was hard to watch and do nothing to help Dusty.

But, the man had to do this on his own. He needed to kill Titus because that monster had tortured and killed Elijah, his son.

Dusty seemed to feel no pain; he finally had Titus by the throat. He shook violently from left to right until the bastard didn't move anymore. Then, I heard a loud roar, which could only mean one thing, Igor was here as well.

There was fighting near the front desk, and I saw Lamar pulling a wolf shifter away from a nurse. My mate hadn't shifted but had remained in his human form. I must admit that it was hot to see Lamar fight. Then I felt a searing pain, and it was like my back was on fire. "What the hell?" I growled as I turned and saw the freaking tiger shifter, syringe in hand.

I don't know what he thought when he injected me, but when I didn't go down, his eyes filled with fear. "Too late to be afraid, bastard," I growled as I grabbed him by the throat. Somehow, I changed from my first form into my second one without noticing. I squeezed the life out of the tiger and threw him away like trash, which he was.

Should I feel different after that idiot had injected me with God only knew what? Then, I changed back into my first form, then into my second form again. What the hell was happening to me? Doctor Krause, who had found the syringe, had identified the contents. "It's a sedative that should knock you off your feet. Your tiger is preventing that from happening by changing back and forth. Don't resist; it seems that your tiger knows what to do to keep you safe," Doctor Krause said. That's when I stopped resisting and let my tiger handle it.

It was a strange feeling to notice my tiger take control, in a good way this time. Even though I still was changing into my first and second form, I managed to look around. The fighting had stopped. I didn't see Dusty, but he would be in Vera's room. Lamar and my father were watching me with interest.

"Where's is Igor?" I asked because I didn't see him anywhere. However, his scent was all over the place, so I knew that he had been there. "It looks like he got away, again," Lamar growled. My tiger finally stopped changing forms. "Thank you for helping us," Doctor Krause said as he glanced around. The entrance windows were shattered, and the front desk was broken. In the hall lay dead hyenas, wolves, and tigers. Blood was everywhere.

My father explained why Igor had launched the attack. He was hell bend on getting his hands on Vera Reed. It meant that she wasn't safe at the facility anymore. "We need to bring Vera home to the estate," I said. My father nodded; he said, "Yes because she's not safe here anymore. Neither are the other residents because if Vera stays here, Igor will launch another attack for sure." I agreed, and we couldn't let that happen. I hated that Igor had managed to escape once again. What was he, freaking Houdini?

"Look what we have here?" I turned and saw Dusty, and he dragged an unconscious and bloody Doyle behind him. "Ah, well, at least we have one scumbag who we can interrogate," I said. "Damn right," Dusty growled. I knew that the life of the leader of the hawks was forfeit, and if he regained consciousness, he would know that too.

I suspected that I wouldn't get him to talk using my fists. It didn't matter; I would get him to spill the beans because I had potions and spells. Igor had managed to escape, but my father had wounded him badly. "Doyle must know where Igor has his hiding place. I'll get him to talk; it doesn't matter what it takes," I growled. Igor had escaped for the last time. But no more, we would find him and then kill him. That bastard would never get the chance to harm anyone ever again.

My father and Lamar had called their cleaning crew to help clean the facility so that the residents could let out their rooms again. Dusty had his arm around Vera as they walked toward the car. They would stay at the estate until Igor was captured and killed. Then, Vera would return to The Hope Garden Psychiatric Institution for shifters. It was there that she would get the treatment that she needed.

"What the hell? Where am I," growled Doyle. My father, Lamar, Dusty, and I stood in front of the cage that had once been my, well, prison. My tiger had taken control many times, and I had woken in this cage, afterward, every time. So, I knew that there wasn't any escape possible.

Then, Doyle seemed to notice us, and he growled even harder. I knew he wanted to shift, but one injection from Doctor Belinsky and his hawk was subdued. "What is the meaning of this?" Doyle said as he motioned to the cage he was in. "Well, as you can see, we have captured you, and now you're in this cage," my father said.

"Where am I?" Doyle demanded to know. "You don't need to know," I said. Doyle cocked his head. "What do you mean by that?" "You won't go anywhere because after you tell us everything that we want to know, we will end your miserable existence," I said matter of factly.

Doyle looked thoughtful for a moment; then, he started laughing. I frowned because, what the hell? "Yeah, right? I don't think so," he said, and the man sounded so sure. I eyed my father and Lamar silently, asking for permission to get Doyle to talk. We really needed to know where Igor had his hiding place.

Lamar nodded; I smiled as I rubbed my hands. "Alright, I will start with an easy question," I said. "I won't tell you shit," Doyle spat. "We will see about that," I replied calmly. "First question. Where is Igor Balashov hiding?" Doyle looked the other way as he didn't say anything. "Where is Igor hiding?" I asked again, and this time my tone was more demanding, still no sound from Doyle.

"Well, Doyle, I don't have time for this because I need to speak to Igor." I paused, then used my power to force him to look at me; I said, "Do you know why I want to speak to him so desperately?" Doyle looked at me with so much hatred in his eyes; it should have killed me on the spot. Still, he didn't say anything.

"You see, Igor knows where my mother is because he kept her from her family for over twenty-six years." And now, I didn't hide the tension in my voice. Doyle had noticed it too because suddenly, he didn't look so cocky anymore. The leader of the hawks was getting scared, and he should be. My eyes were glowing, and my face shifted, just my face. There wasn't any other shifter able to do that. Well, not to my knowledge anyway.

"You. You. What are you?" Doyle finally whispered. "I'm your worst nightmare," I told him, my voice flat and icy. "You have two choices, and that's more than Elijah got," I growled. Doyle backed away. "We will kill you, no matter what happens. However, we can do it slowly, which would take days or months even. Or, we can make it a quick one. It's totally up to you."

"I wasn't planning on torturing Doyle because that was not who I was. Nor my father or Lamar would torture the bastard. So we left the room, leaving a screaming Doyle behind.

"He won't talk, that's for sure," I said. "That means that you need a spell. And I just finished one that would be perfect for you to use on Doyle," Grandma Natalya said. I sensed Grandma Anichka's tension and no wonder. Grandma Anichka Gurkovsky Vasiliev was my mother's mother. So, it was only natural that she was on edge. If we managed to find Igor, we would make him talk. Igor would tell us where he had hidden my mother, Nadia, Vasiliev Balashov all those years

The thought of Igor taking me away from my mother and dumping me with the Jennings had my blood boiling. I know that when I got my hands on him, I would show him no mercy. He hadn't shown my mother or me any mercy when he had separated us. But, then, the bastard let my father believe that his mate and newborn son had died. How could someone be so cruel? To make matters worse, the man was family.

Chapter 27

"Now, let's see if this spell lets you sing like a canary. My grandmother wrote it especially for you. So, that's quite an honor." I glanced at him, smiling evilly. "Do you have anything to say before I cast the spell?" I asked in a very calm voice. Doyle's expression was one of fear. It seemed that he only now saw the danger he was in. Maybe he had expected that Igor would rescue him?

"He's not coming, you know. Igor, I mean. He won't come to your rescue because he's terrified of my father. And of course, he would have my mate and me to deal with too," I explained. I was looking bored because it would make Doyle even more uncomfortable.

I was right when I saw Doyle swallowing hard, and then he started to sweat, which was odd. Shifters didn't sweat, yet, here he was sweating like a pig. "Alright, this won't hurt, I promise," I said in a condescending tone I would use reassuring a small child who is afraid of needles. I knew it would tick the man off because this was a massive insult.

"Now now. Calm down; it will be over before you know it," I said. My grandmother had handed me the spell, which I had modified a bit. I wanted the asshole dead, this spell would probably fry his brain, and I couldn't care less.

No one knew that I was with Doyle. I knew that this would get me in big trouble with my father and with my mate. I opened the bag I had brought with me, unpacked its contents. "What the hell?" Doyle growled. I didn't acknowledge him but began to put six blue candles in a circle around the cage. Blue is the color of the sky and stands for wisdom, faith, truth, confidence, loyalty, and heaven. So it's a powerful color.

When I was done placing the candles, I placed an Onyx gemstone behind each candle. Onyx stands for strength, defense, and protection. Now, it was time for the spell.

"What are you doing? I have rights," Doyle yelled. I ignored him because it was too late for him to start talking, which I was sure he wouldn't do. Instead, I took four gemstones in my hand, looked up, and began the spell.

I turned to the north; I call Earth; I placed the Jade on the floor. I turned to the east; I call Water; I placed the Rose Quartz on the floor. I turned to the west; I call Air and placed the Topaz on the floor. I turned to the south; I call Fire; I placed the Opal on the floor. Then, started repeating.

I call earth, I call Water, I call Air, and I call fire.
Let the truth be said, that's my heart's desire.
To see the truth and to know the way, I call Freya, Ester, and Medea.
By the power of three, open Doyle's mind, let his secrets be revealed, so mote it be.

I needed to repeat the spell three more times before Doyle grabbed his head, trying to keep his secrets, but it was to no avail. Then he started talking, and once he started, he couldn't stop. He told me about Paulina, Titus' daughter, and how he wanted to claim her as his mate. Titus had promised Doyle that he could get Paulina if he would swear his loyalty to the hyenas. So, by that union, the hawks would be obliged to do Titus' bidding.

The bastard had said yes to the deal, much to my disgust. Doyle knew where Igor had his hiding place. My heart skipped a few beats because it wouldn't take long now before I would find my mother.

Doyle had spilled the beans and had answered all of my questions. Now it was time to let him go, as in meeting his maker. I eyed Doyle for a few seconds. "It's time for you to meet your maker," I softly said. He wouldn't feel a thing; even though I would kill him, I wasn't a psychopath. I didn't kill for fun, only if it was necessary.

Now that the truth is heard and said, remove all the memories from Doyle's head.
Hear my plea, power of three, so mote it be.

Doyle looked at me; then he fell; the bastard was dead before he hit the floor.

I rushed outside and drove away before anyone would see me. No one knew that I had sneaked into the barn and cast a truth spell on Doyle. I drove fast and straight to the cottage where I knew I would find Igor.

I parked the car about two miles from the cottage because, as a shifter, Igor had a superior hearing. Even though the man was a psychopath, he wasn't an idiot. *"Baby? Where are you? Are you okay?"* Shit, they must have found Doyle. *"I'm fine. I'll be home soon with a present,"* I told my mate.

"You have to come back right away, baby," Lamar pleaded. *"Soon,"* I replied before I closed the mind link. It

hurt when I pushed my mate out, but I had no choice. I needed to focus on capturing Igor and bringing him to the mansion.

"I felt Lamar push, trying to reactivate our mind link. I built the wall in my head even higher to prevent my mate from getting through to me. Now I could concentrate on my dear Great Uncle Igor. It was about time that that bastard would take responsibility for what he had done. Igor must know that once we captured him, he wouldn't survive.

I slowly crept toward the cabin, where I knew I would find Igor. I was careful to watch that the wind wouldn't betray my approach. To stay against the wind was best because that way, Igor would never sense me. If anything, he would only be able to hear me. So, I moved very carefully toward the cabin.

I saw smoke coming from the chimney, so the bastard was home, good. Unfortunately, I didn't have a spell ready to overpower him, which meant that it would come to a fight. I knew that Igor wouldn't roll over and play dead, no, not him.

I managed to sneak up to the window that was the living room. Igor sat in front of the fireplace, and he was wounded. My father had told me that even though Igor had managed to get away, he had wounded the man. I wondered why he hadn't shifted yet because that would speed up the healing process.

Suddenly Igor lifted his head; he looked from left to right. Shit, the man was listening. Or could he scent me? I only now noticed that there wasn't any wind, damn and double damn. Igor stood and walked over and looked out

the window I was hiding under. I held my breath; it
wouldn't do me any good if he would discover me right
now.

Well, no such luck. "Mitchell, you bastard, I know that
you're here. I know that you can hear me, so listen, and
listen good to what I have to say," he said. Well, I didn't
have another choice. Igor kept standing in front of the
window, which meant I couldn't retreat.

"Alexei thinks that you are his son. He desperately
wants you to be his son. But, unfortunately, you're not
his." There was a pause. The following words shocked the
hell out of me. "You are my son," Igor finally said.

Before I knew what I was doing, I jumped up, shifted
into my second form, and scattered the window. It was
evident that whatever Igor had expected, this wasn't it.
"What the hell?" Igor growled. I saw that he was on the
verge of shifting. But he was severely wounded, and
because of that, it took time. I had him by the throat before
the first hairs could sprout.

"Oh no, you bastard, monster. You're not going
anywhere but home to take responsibility for everything
that you did." Igor opened his mouth, probably to protest
or something, but I shut him down hard. "Ah ah. Not a
word," I growled deep and low. Something in my eyes
must have warned him because, to my astonishment, he
closed his mouth again.

"You will go home to face judgment, but not before
you tell me where my mother is. Don't take me for a fool
because I know she's not dead. Also, I'm not your son; my
mother would have never cheated on her mate, my father,"
I growled while I tightened the grip I had on his throat.

When he was gasping for air, I had to loosen my grip. What came next made me realize that Igor was even more psychopath than I had anticipated. He looked at me, gave me a sickening smile, and said, "I forced Nadia; she didn't volunteer."

I don't know how I managed to stay calm and focused, but I did; what the hell was wrong with the bastard. Did he have a death wish? Then it hit me, Jesus Christ, he had a death wish. Igor kept looking and smiling. "You should kill me for raping your mother. You should kill me for kidnapping her and abusing her nearly every day. For keeping you from her, and for me, being your father," Igor kept talking about how I should kill him because he had done those terrible things.

I stared right back, and my smile was maybe even eviler than his. "I'm not your son. You never raped my mother. You took her from us, yes, but you never touched her." I pulled him closer, so we were almost nose to nose. "I could kill you here, on the spot, but I'm not going to do that." Igor still smiled, still had that eerie gleam in his eyes. It was an odd glare that only the worst psychopaths had.

"Before I take you to my father, so you can face justice, you're going to tell me where my mother is," I growled, and I felt my eyes begin to glow. I knew that it was a spooky sight because I was told many times that it was scary as hell.

Igor's eyes widened in shock; it seemed that even a psychopath like him could get scared. Even so, the bastard kept his lip tightly pressed together. It looked like he wouldn't talk, damn. My father had warned me that Igor would be hard to crack. That the chances he would talk were slim to none. Well, my father had been right because the situation Igor was in should have made him spill the beans. Yet, here we were, my appearance must have been scary, but Igor, who genuinely seemed afraid, kept his mouth shut.

Chapter 28

"Baby, don't you ever do that to me again," Lamar said. I had nearly squeezed the life out of Igor. I could do so because the man was severely wounded. Plus, my tiger had partly taken control by shifting in my second form and grabbed Igor by the throat before the man knew what was happening.

When Igor was unconscious, I had called Lamar to pick me up because it was too risky to drive home with Igor in the trunk. I wouldn't make the mistake of underestimating him, again. Now, Igor was in the cage that had held Doyle. There was no way he would be able to escape.

We had tried to get Igor to talk, but no such luck just as my father had predicted. Igor would be a hard nut to crack. I wanted the truth spell I had used on Doyle, use on Igor too. But Grandma Natalya had said that it would be a bad idea. So she and Grandma Anichka would write a new one. The truth spell I had used on Doyle hadn't been that powerful. To get Igor to talk, we would need one that was ten times more powerful.

"Promise me that you won't ever do that again. I know that you're very powerful, but so is Igor. Plus, Igor fights dirty. I need your word on this," Lamar urged. "I won't," I promised as I pulled Lamar close and nibbled his earlobe. My mate moaned softly, and that was exactly how I wanted it. I started unbuttoning his shirt and licked and sucked every inch of flesh that became available with every button I opened. "God, yes. Feels so good," Lamar moaned as he began to move his hips slowly. The move was so damn sexy that it made me rip his shirt open in one swift move. "Oh my. So eager. I love that I have that effect on you," Lamar said as he lifted me and threw me on the bed.

My mate used shifter speed to get both of us naked in seconds; I loved it when he did that. "I need you," I panted as I wrapped my hand around my shaft and slowly started stroking myself. Lamar was watching me intently, and his erection grew even bigger. The man's cock was massive, and my mouth went dry.

"You are so beautiful. So hot and so damn sexy," I paused and added, grinning, "And intelligent too." "Spread your leg for me, baby." I did as I was told, and Lamar inserted two fingers at once. "Yes, oh yes," I moaned as I started to rock my hips in anticipation.

Because we had sex all the time, I didn't really need preparation, but Lamar knew that I loved the foreplay. So I spread my legs as wide as I could. Lamar added a third finger, and when he touched my sweet spot, I went nuts. I was bucking my hips so frantically that Lamar had to stop with what he was doing and put both hands on my hips.

"Easy, baby. I don't want you to hurt yourself,' he whispered hoarsely. I looked him in his beautiful ocean blue eyes and whispered, "Fuck me. I need to feel you inside of me. Fuck me like there's no tomorrow, please?"

Lamar didn't reply; instead, he pulled his fingers back, grabbed and positioned his cock, and then he pushed in, hard. "That's it. That's how I like it," I whispered when Lamar was pushing in hard, pulling back slowly, taking his time. Then, he drove in hard again; yes, the man did know how to drive me crazy.

I grabbed Lamar's hair and, slowly, very slowly, pulled him toward me while we kept staring into each other's eyes. For a moment, time seemed to stand still; Lamar, who was entirely inside me, didn't move. Then I slammed our mouths together. Lamar parted his lips immediately, and not waiting for an invitation; I shoved my tongue inside.

"Move. For God's sake, move," I growled, and Lamar did. This time he used more force, and it was heaven, as he pushed in and pulled out faster and faster. I fisted the sheets because I had to grab something. Then I slung my arms around Lamar's neck and started moving my hips, so we moved in unison.

Lamar was pounding into me with so much force, and he was kissing and nibbling my neck, collarbone, and he even managed to pinch my nipple playfully. The man was a God; it was that simple. I was losing my rhythm. "Oh-oh, close, so close. I need to," that was a far as I got. Lamar watched in awe as hot wet seamen splashed between our bodies.

Lamar once had told me that he would never get enough of watching me come. I knew that Lamar was on edge as well when he lost his rhythm as well. "Come for me, my mate. Give me all you got," I panted.

"That was just what I needed," I softly said, still catching my breath. Yes, even we shifters need to catch our breath after a wild session of lovemaking. It wasn't always like this, but at that moment, we had needed it both. The previous night it had been slow lovemaking, which I also loved. "I love and adore you, baby," Lamar said as he leaned in and kissed me. It was a gentle kiss, full of emotion. "I love and adore you too, my mate," I returned. We kissed again and this time with more passion and urgency. We lay side by side for a while; no words were needed.

I opened my eyes; something had woken me, but what. It was dark outside, so it was still early. I glanced sideways; my mate was fast asleep. So, what had me wake up? I slid out of bed and had to be careful because I didn't want to wake Lamar.

I stood in front of the window and glanced into the darkness. Everything seemed peaceful, so why wasn't I asleep? Then I heard it; somewhere nearby, a wolf was howling. It was a howling full of sorrow and pain. What the hell?

"Vera, shit!" Lamar said. I turned and saw Lamar disappear. I hadn't even noticed that he was awake. I put on my sweatpants and ran after Lamar. When I left the room, I saw Dusty coming out of his room, and he, too, was running. "What the hell is going on?" my father questioned. Dimitri and Felix stood in front of their bedroom, watching the scene unfold. It was chaos because Arkady came up the stairs, checking on my father and me. Arkady's first priority was to defend my father and me.

"It's Vera; we heard howling. I don't know what's wrong, but whatever it is, it's not good," I said. "Call the doctor," Lamar yelled, and to my astonishment, Arkady grabbed his phone and was already dialing.

"How is she?" I asked Lamar. It was morning, and we sat at the table drinking coffee. Even though my two grandmothers had cooked a delicious breakfast, no one was hungry. "We don't know. Physically she should completely recover. However, her mental condition is much worse. She doesn't want to live anymore. It looks like she has given up. And because of that, her body might not heal. This is because the body, mind, and soul are tightly connected, especially for us shifters," Lamar explained.

I understood what my mate meant. Shifters were one with their spirit, body, and soul. Vera had experienced a tremendous loss when Elijah was tortured to death. She had felt her son's pain and had heard him screaming for her to, please, help him. That should be enough for anyone to fall into the abyss, mentally. Unfortunately, Vera had fallen deep, and there was no guarantee that she would climb out of the bottomless dark pit.

It seemed that her wolf had given up as well because I had carefully tried to sense it. Unfortunately, I couldn't detect her spirit, which was a bad sign. The animal had retreated, and we could only hope that in time, it would surface again. It was because her spirit had given up that Vera had been able to slice her throat. Otherwise, her wolf would have stopped her. Instead, however, we had heard it howl in pain, sorrow, and regret.

I sighed deeply; one thing was sure, we had captured Igor, and he wouldn't get away alive. Doyle and the Karr brothers were dead; only Igor was left. For a moment, I thought about letting him suffer just as we had. But then again, we weren't psychopaths. So, his death would be quick.

No one knew it, but I had written a very powerful spell to make Igor talk. However, in the end, it would fry his brain, just like the spell I had used on Doyle. Well, since he would die anyway, it didn't matter.

Dusty was with his mate, Grandma Anichka had
brought him coffee and breakfast, but he hadn't touched it.
I saw the tray untouched when I was on my way to the
bedroom to shower and dress. Shit, this was so not good,
and I hoped that we wouldn't lose Dusty in the process. As
long as Vera was breathing, Dusty would too. But, the
moment Vera's heart would stop, then the chances of
Dusty surviving were slim to none.

I needed to find a way to save Vera, but how? My
grandmothers had warned me not to try and heal her mind.
Vera was fragile, and even more now that she had tried to
end her life. I had wanted to take a look at Dusty, maybe I
could lessen his grief, but again, my grandmothers had
warned me to stay out of it. They told me to trust the fates
and not interfere. I had to give them my word that I
wouldn't.

Grandma Anichka and Grandma Natalya knew me all
too well. And, when I gave them my word, they knew that
I would keep it. Then, Lamar wanted my word that I would
never take off like I had done to catch Igor. Or to handle
Igor on my own. So, I gave him my word too.

I showered, dressed, and went downstairs to join my
father, Arkady, and Lamar when they would interrogate
Igor. I had my spell ready, but since I gave my word, I
would inform them about the spell I wrote. Of course, I had
to explain that it would, in the end, fry his brain.

Ronan, the hawk, was doing very well after a second
and third healing session. He told me that as of now, he
would manage to recover on his own. However, I let him
know that I would be there for him if he needed me. Ronan
was staying at my father's estate too. Well, for the time

being, because it still was too dangerous for him to return
home.

Chapter 29

Two days had passed since I had captured Igor.
Grandma Natalya had completed brewing the potion that
would strip Igor of his tiger. The beast would disappear
completely, which meant Igor's inevitable death. A shifter
couldn't survive without his spirit, well, not for long
anyway. If a shifter lost their animal, it would drive him
mad.

Dusty still hadn't left Vera's room, and it wasn't a
good sign. The shifter also hadn't touched his food, which
wasn't good either. I was worried because, as a pack, we
were close; we were family. Now, two of that family
members were suffering because of Igor.

"I wish that there was something we could do to help
Dusty and Vera," I softly said when we walked toward the
barn where Igor was held. Lamar's smile was rueful when
he answered, "I know, baby. I know. Right now, there's
nothing that we can do. It's in fate's hands; we can only
hope."

Igor growled when he saw us enter the barn. I observed
Arkady after all he once had called Igor his friend. Well,
not so much now, judging by the man's expression. I was
excited, nervous, and full of rage at the same time. Lamar
touched my shoulder. *"Concentrate. Stay calm. You need
to stay calm and keep control over your tiger. If you don't,
then it will attack and kill Igor before we can question the
bastard."*

I inhaled and exhaled a few times and finally calmed down. My tiger had become restless because my emotions were all over the place. Now it calmed down as well. It looked like I finally controlled my tiger, and the thought hit me like a ton of bricks. Lamar smiled knowingly.

We all stood in front of the cage at a certain distance when my father took a step forward. "So, Igor," he began, and I noticed that his tone was mild. "You know why you're here." Igor stared daggers at me, addressed me when he replied. "Go to hell, all of you. I will never tell you where to find her." The words were so full of hatred that they even got me off guard.

"Oh, but that's where you're wrong, Igor," Nicolay Balashov, my grandfather, answered instead of my father. My grandfather wasn't a man of many words so that he replied instead of my father was rare. Igor glanced at my grandfather. "What are you doing here? You, as my brother, should stand by my side and not side with that trash," he said as he pointed at us.

"You are the trash, not them," my grandfather replied coolie. "Now, tell us where Nadia is. And I believe that you also know what happened to Borya Vasiliev," my grandfather inquired, his tone icy, which gave even me the creeps.

Igor smiled, and it wasn't a pleasant one. "Why do you think I had anything to do with Borya's disappearance?" "I don't think, I know, that you are responsible for the man's disappearance," my grandfather said. Igor considered him for a while, then he said teasingly. "Well, you might be right." My grandmother gasped because her mate had been missing for more than thirty years. So, to hear that Igor might be involved in Borya's missing came as a bit of a shock. But, it also would mean that she finally would find out what had happened to her mate.

"Make no mistake. We can force you to talk, and we will. Now is the time to redeem what's left of your soul. Think about it, but not too long," my grandfather was on a roll; I've never heard him speak so much.

"I see you all in hell before I tell you where Nadia and Borya are," Igor spat out. Then, the bastard unleashed his tiger. "Oh, hell. What's happening?" I yelled as I grabbed my throat. It felt like I couldn't breathe. "That's Igor's power, and be glad that he's wounded, or else it would be much worse,' my grandfather panted. It was obvious that Grandpa Nicolay didn't suffer as much from the lack of oxygen as I had.

Just when I thought I would black out, my tiger roared in rage. It was helping me to breathe. Then it was over, and I could breathe normally again. Igor had unleashed his tiger, hoping to escape the cage he was in. Well, what he didn't know was that this particular cage was designed to keep me in. When I first started shifting, I had trouble controlling my tiger. It's never good when a tiger is on the loose. That's why my father had built this special cage, which was strong enough to hold my tiger. So, it was certainly strong enough to keep Igor's tiger contained.

I looked at Grandma Natalya; she nodded as she fished a piece of paper out of her bag. I took the bag and retrieved the candles, crystals, and herbs. I placed the white candles in a circle while I kept chanting the words, *by the power of he, by the power of she, by the power of three.* Then, I put the crystals in place; they would form the outer circle. If the candles failed to contain the power of Igor, the crystals would for sure.

Igor would try to break free, and even though the candles were powerful, we didn't take any risk. Even though he was wounded, Igor could still pose a danger. The power that he unleashed just now had been proof of that.

Igor roared in rage when he saw what I was doing. It was now that he recognized the dire situation he was in. Igor knew that Grandma Natalya was a powerful witch. And with the help of Grandma Anichka, even though she wasn't a witch, the women were almost unstoppable.

I glanced at Igor while I was burning the sage. Yes, he had never expected this, of that I was sure. Nevertheless, I smiled when I told him that I had killed Doyle and that the man had betrayed him by telling me about Igor's hiding place. "Without Doyle's help, I probably never would have found you," I said as I mixed the burned sage with lavender.

"You bastard," Igor yelled as he threw himself against the bars of the cage. I ignored him when I sprinkled the mixed herbs in a circle behind the crystals. "Are you done, kotyonok?" "Yes." The only thing that we needed to do was feed Igor the potion that would magnify the spell. "Doctor Belinsky, if you would do the honors?" my father said. "With pleasure," the doctor replied as he stared daggers at Igor.

The doctor had seen the horrible things Igor had done, and that's why he didn't have a problem sedating Igor so we could feed him the potion. "What are you doing? Don't. Stay away from me, you filthy piece of shit," Igor was panicking. "Game Over, you lose," I said, and then Doctor Belinsky aimed the gun that contained a tranquilizer and fired. Before Igor knew what happened, he went down, hard.

Grandma Natalya held out her hand, and I took it. She held the piece of paper so we could read it both, and then we started chanting the spell. It was a powerful spell that should banish Igor's tiger once and for all.

We say this spell and call upon fate tonight.
We are witch and wizard; we stand and fight.
Igor Balashov, see the cruelty, see the pain.
See the suffering that you cost, over and over again.
To part from your tiger is your fate.
Let him travel through time and space.
He now shall leave Igor Balashov and this place.
We call Sophie, Faith, and Grace.
Take Igor's tiger and leave this place.

Even though he was sedated, Igor began to scream, and then we saw his tiger emerge. This should not be possible. It just showed how powerful Igor really was. I also realized that I had put my life in danger by going after Igor by myself.

Not only Igor, but his tiger had the same madness shining in his eyes. Grandma Natalya and I repeated the spell three times. Finally, with one last deafening roar, Igor's tiger was gone.

I was exhausted, as was Grandma Natalya, but we didn't have time to rest, not yet. Igor was weak, and now was the time to get him to talk. We needed to act fast because there was no telling when Igor would go over the edge. A shifter couldn't survive without his animal. Igor lost his tiger, and since he already was unstable, he could go gaga every moment.

"Igor," I said in a commanding voice. Igor looked up, his eyes were open, but the lights were out. Then, to everyone's astonishment, he spoke. "I'll die before I tell you where Nadia is." When my father had told me that Igor would never talk, he hadn't exaggerated.

"He will talk," I growled because I still had the spell I wrote, especially for Igor. I had told my family about the spell, so they knew what I meant. "Do it," my grim-looking father said. I could tell that the man was on edge.

Hear my call, hear my cry, spirits from the other side.
To me, Igor's mind has no secrets to hide.
Lift the veil from my eyes.
Show me what Igor hides.
By the power of three, I conjure thee.
To reveal the truth to me.

The loss of his tiger had weakened Igor, and that's the only reason I didn't need to repeat the spell.

"What did you say?" my father's voice was low and deadly. "I keep Nadia at the Finch Place," Igor repeated. He began to slur, a clear sign that he was at the end of his sanity. Soon he would go over the edge.

Igor started laughing, although it didn't really sound like laughing. "I keep Borya there as well. All this time, they were right under your nose, and you didn't have a clue," Igor laughed even harder. To know that his mate had been in Serigala Valley all this time drove my father over the edge before Igor lost it completely.

The Finch Place was on the outskirts of Serigala Valley, not far from my father's estate. Before I could interfere, my father had opened the cage. He put his hands around Igor's neck and choked him.

Chapter 30

"Hell no!" my father growled. It was a disaster; the man had killed Igor way too soon. It turned out that the Finch Place was protected with several spells. So, we knew where my mother and Grandfather Borya were, but we couldn't reach them. Soon, my father would go bonkers. Who could blame him?

For twenty-six years, he had believed that his mate was dead. That she died in childbirth, that he also had lost his son. Igor had let him believe that I had been stillborn. Now he had found me, and together we had hunted for Igor, forcing him to reveal the truth about my mother. Now, we stood in front of the Finch Place and couldn't enter. The spells and wards were powerful. We needed Grandma Natalya and Grandma Anichka to come up with a powerful counterspell.

"So close, and yet so far away," Lamar whispered. I nodded because the lump in my throat prevented me from talking. We need to undo those God damned spells," I growled. My mother was in there, and we couldn't get to her because Igor had secured the place like Fort Knox. And how must Grandma Anichka feel? Her mate, who had been missing for thirty years, was in there as well. She appeared calm, but I knew that she was anything but—the poor woman.

My father looked white as a sheet, and I understood. Yes, we really needed to reverse the spells fast. "They aren't as complicated as you might think." For a moment, I was stunned, as was my father. "Yuri? What are you doing here? You should be home, where you're safe," I murmured. The boy smiled. "No, Uncle Mitch, I'm right where I need to be," the kid replied.

I smiled because the boy had called me uncle. It was the first time that he called me uncle. I know that it might sound silly, but at that moment, I felt ten feet tall. Then Yuri moved until he stood directly in front of the house. No one said a word. My Uncle Andrei, Yuri's father, was standing beside me. He shook his head when I opened my mouth to ask him about his son. I closed my mouth again.

I tried to talk to my mate via our mind link, but he had closed himself off. Lamar looked at me and smiled apologetically; now, I understood. We knew that Yuri was very sensitive to his surroundings. So, there was a possibility that he would sense Lamar and me using our mind link. I didn't exactly know what it was that Yuri was doing, but we didn't want to disturb him.

Yuri was special; of that I was convinced. Unfortunately, my Uncle Andrei, Yuri's father, seemed to have trouble getting used to the idea that his son is special. It seemed like forever when Yuri finally turned to face us. The boy's expression made me fear for the worst, and I was right.

"The cabin is tightly secured with wards and spells, which are very powerful." Yuri paused. Then, he smiled, and his eyes twinkled when he added. "To break down the wards and undo the spells will be difficult. But it's not impossible."

I smiled. "alright, that's good news, Yuri. What do you need from us?" I questioned. Because, unlike Uncle Andrei, I trusted the boy's abilities. It wasn't that Andrei didn't like it that his son was special. No, it was more like the man didn't know how to deal with it. Thank God, Katarina, Yuri's mother, and Andrei's mate didn't have that problem. She knew they just needed to accept Yuri as he was and love him.

Love, unconditional love, was even more important than acceptance. And the boy was loved by Andrei and Katarina; their love was unconditional. It was what Yuri needed, and I had told Uncle Andrei so when he had come to me for advice. After all, I was special too, even though I didn't feel that way. It was the same with Yuri; the boy didn't feel special, which was good. That way, he would stay humble.

Andrei gazed from his son to me and back to Yuri again. He surprised me when he spoke. "Tell us what you need, son. We will provide it for you." Yuri's smile was so bright it could light up a huge city for a whole night. "We need Grandma Anichka because Grandpa Borya is in the cabin. We need her love to break down the wards." Yuri eyed my father and me; he said, "We need the two of you because Nadia, your mate," Yuri looked at my father. "And you," he eyed me, "Are her son. It will be your love combined that will tear down most of the wards."

"Also, we will need Grandma Natalya because she has to write some powerful, ass-kicking spells that override the ones who are in place now." Yuri looked at his father, and it warmed my soul when I saw the pride and adoration in the man's eyes. He was proud of Yuri, making the boy grow ten feet tall. Katarina smiled and nodded in approval.

Andrei loved his son unconditionally, and now, there was acceptance as well. It was all Yuri needed to grow up and embrace his powers. Often, when one or both parents couldn't accept that their child was special, the kid could end up hating the gift he had received. It was then that such a child would become unstable and lose his sanity. That would make the kid very dangerous. Thank God, Yuri and I had parents who loved and accepted us just like we were.

Well, for now, it was only my father, but I was sure that my mother would love me no matter what. After all, she herself was part witch; even if she was just a shifter, I knew that her love would be unconditional. I felt it deep in my soul.

My father still hadn't said a word, and that worried me. He was staring at the cottage, looking pale. "Are you okay?" I asked when I was next to him. "No," he said. His answer was clipped; he didn't even look at me when he answered. Instead, the man kept staring at the house where he knew he would find his mate, my mother, Nadia Vasiliev Balashov.

Grandma Natalya had gone back to the estate to start working on a spell. We had to get her first, so she could, with Yuri's help, identify the spells and wards. I had gone back to the estate as well because we needed to eat and drink.

When I returned with baskets filled with sandwiches, fruit, meat, and other things, I noticed that my father was standing in the same spot. I sighed because the man had to eat and drink. "Dad? You need to eat something," I softly said. Arkady and Andrei had unpacked the food. "I'm not hungry," he replied without looking away from the cottage.

"Dad, it won't do anyone any good if you starve yourself. You need your strength because my mother will need you after freeing her. You will need all your strength to guide mother back to reality. We don't know how she is doing or if she knows for how long she was at the cabin," I said. When I had said reality, I was careful not to mention sanity.

My words had seemed to penetrate my father's mind because he slowly took the sandwich I held out to him. Even though he had eaten the whole sandwich, I still was worried. Hell, for more than twenty-six years, the man believed that his mate and son were dead. Now he knew different, as he was standing in front of the cabin where my mother was imprisoned.

Many of the Balashov Streak and even the pack wanted to come to support my father, which was very nice. It also showed that the wolves and tigers had bonded well. Lamar had thanked them but explained that only a few were allowed to be present for now. Arkady had told the tigers the same.

We knew that it would take a while for Grandma Natalya to come up with a, as Yuri called it, kick-ass spell. But, even so, my father didn't want to leave. I understood because I felt the same. It was like when we would leave; my mother would disappear. Who knew, maybe she would, but we would never find out because we wouldn't leave.

Grandma Anichka was with us as well; she, too, refused to leave. Not now she was so close to getting back her mate, after thirty years. She, too, was pale and quiet and kept gazing at the cottage. I felt for my father and my grandmother.

"Grandma Anichka?" Yuri said in a soft voice as if he was afraid to scare her. "Yes, Yuri." Shall we start tearing down those damn wards?" Even though the boy had spoken softly, we all had heard the words.

Yuri held out his hand, and Anichka took it without hesitation. Together they walked closer to the cottage. I felt the grieve and loss my grandmother had suffered. Still, she was so strong, never pitied herself, always had positive thoughts. Now, her eyes were filled with tears as she concentrated on the wards. Yuri's eyes were closed; he let his power flow into Grandma Anichka. When their powers combined, blue and yellow sparks flew from their bodies and surrounded them.

"What the?" Lamar whispered. "Protection. The fire, it's protecting them," I whispered in awe, interrupting my mate. My father still hadn't said anything. He just stood, watching Grandma Anichka and Yuri. Andrei and Katarina were observing their son intently.

Grandma Anichka and Yuri stood for quite some time, just whispering what I assumed must be an incantation. They still were holding hands, then they raised their hands, and the fire that surrounded them intensified. The silence was deafening; even the birds had stopped singing. It was eerie.

I gasped when I saw the wards becoming visible. I'd never seen wards like these before. Wards protected every window and the doors. The wards all looked the same, but when I looked closer, I saw that every single one was different. It was subtle, but nevertheless, I noticed it.

Red and black strands were twisted around each other. It looked like it was jumbled up or something. However, when I kept staring at it, I noticed that there seemed to be a pattern. Yes, there was a pattern I was sure of it. So I assumed that Grandma Anichka and Yuri had also seen it. Suddenly Grandma Anichka began to draw in front of her. She stopped abruptly, but then Yuri whispered something I couldn't hear, and Grandma Anichka began to draw in the air again.

"Love, opened up, grandmother. Unleash the love, the grief, and the sorrow that you felt for more than thirty years," I heard Yuri whisper. I saw her shoulders shake right before she lifted her head and let out a howl that made me cry. I couldn't help it. For a moment, I thought that I felt the earth moving, then it started raining.

"The angels hear you, and they are weeping because they feel your pain and loss, your anger and tremendous suffering over losing your mate," Yuri softly said. That was what Yuri had meant when he had said that he needed Grandma Anichka for her love.

Yuri motioned for my father and me to join them. We walked up to them, and I took Grandma Anichka's hand and squeezed it lightly in silent support. My father took my hand, and together we stared at the wards. Yuri kept looking at the wards when he said, "Uncle Alexei, and Uncle Mitch, unleash your love, grief, sorrow, and loss."

Grandma Anichka kept drawing in the air. The sky had opened up even more; it was pouring now. "The angels are weeping for you too," said Yuri, and I believed him. Grandma Anichka's movements became more frantic. She was drawing very fast now. Then, I saw it. Slowly, very slowly, the wards were unraveled.

Chapter 31

"Finally, the spell is ready," Grandma Natalya said as she filled her mug with coffee. It was the following morning, and Lamar and I were the only ones left. Everyone else was already at the Finch Place. My father had stayed there all night, which was understandable. I wouldn't have left either if it were about Lamar.

I had packed breakfast for my father because it seemed that I was the only one who got him to eat something. When we arrived at the cottage, Yuri and Grandma Anichka were already working to remove the last wards. At midnight Yuri and Grandma Anichka had called it a day because both had been exhausted.

About two hours after we arrived, the last wards were taken down, and Grandma Natalya and I could start to undo the spells. Yuri was also needed now because, well, he saw the spells; I don't know how else to explain. It was how Grandma Natalya had produced a potion so quickly. Two days, it had taken her only two days to come up with the perfect spell. Yuri would point out the spells so Grandma Natalya could aim at the right spot.

Some spells were tricky because you had to hit them right in the center to undo them. These spells were that tricky; thank God that we had Yuri. Before we started to undo the spells, I had to see how my father was holding up. I wonder if he had gotten some sleep at all. He looked terrible.

"Hi, dad. How are you holding up?" I got the answer I already expected. "I'm fine, Mitchell. I only need access to the house so that I can get my mate," he replied. "And mine," Grandma Anichka softly said. My heart broke for these two people I loved and respected so much. Even though we had been in front of the cottage, we hadn't seen my mother or Grandfather Borya. It must be the spell that prevented us from seeing inside the cottage.

"Mitchell, why don't you and your grandmother start undoing the spell," my father softly said. His eyes were on the cottage. I nodded because it was time to break down the last barrier that kept us from my mother and Grandpa Borya.

I looked at my grandmother. "Are you ready to use your kick-ass spells?" I quietly said. "I sure am," she replied in an equally quiet voice. We moved until we stood in front of the door. We would start with the front door. We hoped that we would gain access to the cottage if we undid the spell that blocked the door.

I held Grandma Natalya's right hand, and she held the potion in her left. I held my potion in my right hand. After the spell, we would throw the potion simultaneously at the front door.

We held the piece of paper in our joined hands to read it together. The spell will be at its most powerful if we cast it together. "Ready, kotyonok?" "Yes." "Alright, let's do this."

I want the truth revealed.
I want the secrets unsealed.
By the power of Faith, Sophie, and Grace.
Remove these chains from time and space.

Undo these spells, so they cause no more pain.
Return them to those from where they came.

We said the spell three more times because somehow,
three was a magical number. Then, we simultaneously
threw the potion against the door. Reading a spell three
times made it more powerful. Don't ask me why; it just is.

"The spell still is in place. I feel it," I said after a few
seconds. My grandmother nodded; she had felt it too. My
heart sank when nothing happened, then suddenly a
blinding flash appeared. I had to close my eyes because I
was afraid that it would blind me.

"It's gone. The spell, it's gone," Grandma Natalya
whispered as she stepped forward and grabbed the door
handle. I heard my father gasped and Grandma Anichka
was softly sobbing. My father took her hand, and together
they followed Grandma Natalya inside the cottage.

"Nadia?" my father softly said when he saw a woman
standing near the window. She didn't react, and I knew
then that something was terribly wrong. "Mother? It's me,
Mitchell, your son," I spoke quietly because there was no
saying how she would react. Did she know what was going
on? Was her memory erased?

I was getting worried when she didn't respond to either
of us. She should, at least, react to my father's presence,
but she didn't. It was like she couldn't see us. Like she was
in a different world. That thought his me like a freight
train. "Dad, don't touch her, please don't touch her," I
pleaded.

My father's expression said it all; the man wasn't
planning on listening to me. "Dad, please. Don't touch her;

I believe that she's under a spell," I pleadingly explained. Now, I had his attention. "What do you mean, Mitchell?" my father questioned, and he didn't sound friendly. The man was angry, and even though I knew that his anger wasn't directed at me, I felt guilty as hell.

There, in the corner of the room, stood Alexei Balashov's mate, who he hadn't seen for more than twenty-six years. She didn't react to him, and now he wasn't allowed to touch her? I would have gone bonkers if it were me.

"Tell me, what did you mean by Nadia being under a spell," my father whispered. I knew that if he didn't whisper, he would have screamed. His tiger would have roared in rage. That he managed to keep his animal under control was amazing. It showed how powerful my father was.

"Uncle Alexei?" It was Yuri. "Yes?" "I can see it. Aunt Nadia is under a spell, and this is a nasty one." My mother was staring into space; there was no reaction whatsoever. I could scream. However, I needed to stay calm because my tiger was getting restless. It wouldn't do anyone any good if I lost control again. "We need to get my mother to the estate, but how?" I asked my grandma Natalya.

Suddenly I heard Grandma Anichka yell the name of her mate. "It came from the back," I said as I ran to the back of the place. My father would stay with his mate; that was a given. Arkady would stay with them as well, of that I was sure.

I came to a skidded halt; there, at the backdoor, stood a man who I had only seen in photographs. This must be my other grandfather, the one I hadn't met yet. Grandma Anichka was gasping for air; it was clear that she was shocked. Even though we knew that Grandpa Borya was also in the cottage, Granma Anichka was speechless.

"Borya? Is that really you?" she said in a barely audible tone. To my astonishment, my grandfather responded to her. He looked uncertain. "Anichka Anichka Anichka," he repeated over and over. "Grandfather?" I softly said because I had to do something. He looked at me; he obviously didn't know who I was. "Grandpa? I'm Mitchell, your grandson. I'm the son of Alexei and Nadia," I said.

"This is real. Your mate is standing in front of you. Igor is dead, and so is the rest who were involved in kidnapping you and Nadia, my mother," I explained carefully. Suddenly my grandfather moved to Grandma Anichka and tentatively touched her face. "It is real," he whispered as he hugged the life out of her. Both were crying as they stood there, just holding each other. Grandma Anichka was sobbing quietly into her mate's broad chest.

I silently retreated because this was such an intimate moment. Finally, finally, they were reunited after thirty years of separation. When I returned to my mother's room, I saw that Grandma Natalya was guiding my mother to the front door. My mother, who looked catatonic, let Grandma Natalya guide her to the car. This was so weird, we finally had found my mother, and now the woman didn't recognize either of us. My father was heartbroken and full of rage.

I wanted to resurrect Igor just so I could kill him again, the bastard. What a monster that man had been.

Chapter 32

"Could you repeat that, please," Grandpa Borya whispered; he was shocked, and for a good reason. Grandma Anichka, who was sitting next to her mate, holding his hand, whispered, "Thirty years, my love. Thirty years." She was softly crying, and who could blame her? Grandpa Borya took his mate in his arms and gently rocked her.

Igor's death had been quick, and now I was sorry that I hadn't let him suffer. My heart was breaking at seeing my grandparents' lives destroyed. In time they would be able to function normally again, at least I hoped so.

I eyed my father, and he, too, was heartbroken. One man had cost so much pain and suffering. "I really would like to resurrect Igor, so I can kill him all over again. This time, I would take my time," I growled. My grandmother untangled herself from her mate. Her stare was so intense that it rattled me a bit. She said in a firm voice that was so familiar, "Mitchell, you must never, ever try to bring someone back to life." Seeing my expression, she added, "You can only resurrect someone if you use dark magic. Since you're not a warlock but a wizard, you need to find a warlock who would help you. Or you need to cross over and choose the dark side."

That statement got me completely off guard. I had never thought about dark magic and certainly never thought of practicing it. The thought alone filled me with revulsion. Grandma Anichka had seen it too because she smiled. "I thought so," she said.

My father and I, who had spent time with Grandpa Borya and Grandma Anichka, left the room. What my grandparents needed now the most was privacy. So, everyone was told not to enter the sunroom.

On our way to my mother, we saw Grandma Natalya coming out of her room. She looked so worried and so sad. "How is she?" my father asked in a soft voice. "Still the same. And what's even more concerning, I can't get her to eat. She doesn't react to anything," my grandmother replied.

"How is Borya doing?" she asked my father. "He's responsive, thank God. Now, we need to explain how long he was gone and what happened in those years he wasn't there. But, first, he needs to know about Nadia and Mitchell. Then, we need to ease him into the present because much has changed since he was captured," my father replied. Grandma Natalya nodded.

My father softly knocked at the door before opening it and peeking inside. I felt his pain and agony. Neither my grandmother nor my father had other partners during the time their mates were missing. It told me how loyal my family was.

"Hey, my love," my father said as he gently kissed my mother's temple. She didn't react, which I had expected, but still, it hurt. "Mom?" I said. Still, I got no reaction. I motioned my father to follow me out of the room because we needed to talk.

"What is it?" my father questioned when we were outside in the garden. We had retreated into the garden since we didn't know if my mother would hear everything that was said in her presence. "I want Yuri to take a look at her. Maybe he is able to see why she isn't able to sense us, see us, know that we are here. I suspect that Igor had someone, probably a warlock, cast a spell over mom. It must have been a warlock," I insisted. I knew that if my mother were under a spell, Yuri would be able to see.

My father nodded. "Very well, but I need to ask his parents if they allow it," he replied. "Of course," I said. "We need to see how Vera is doing because now that the threat is over, she can return to The mental facility," my father said. I nodded and could slap myself because, with everything that was going on, I totally had forgotten Vera Reed.

As if reading my thoughts, my father said, "Don't beat yourself up. Even though you have adjusted well and learned a lot, you're still a cub." I didn't like that but knew that the man was right. We walked into the house and stayed in my mother's room for about an hour. We just sat there and talked about everyday things, like my salon and Milo. That Arkady hadn't even liked Milo and me in the beginning. The man hadn't trusted me, and now, he adored us and often took care of Milo when I couldn't.

Grandpa Borya and Grandma Anichka went for a walk in the garden. They had so much to talk about in the days to come. Even though she had her mate back, after thirty years, Grandma Anichka had offered to help with making potions. We still didn't know what was binding my mother. Why she didn't seem aware of us or her surroundings, this is why we needed Yuri. The kid would be able to tell us if my mother was under a spell or whatever.

"Come in," Dusty said before I even had the chance to knock. We entered the room where we saw Vera sitting in a chair that stood by the window, which offered a view over the magnificent garden. "How is she doing? Any changes?" I asked. My father was with me, but she was pack and not a tiger. "Lamar just left," Dusty said. "I know." "Vera is still the same. Her wounds are healing slowly, but." He stopped because it was hard to talk about Vera's situation. She had given up, and that was rare among shifters.

No one actually knew how to deal with that. Doctor Krause did his best, but he was at a loss of how to treat her accordingly. I motioned for Dusty to follow me out of the room and told him what I had discussed with my father. I wanted Dusty's permission to let Yuri take a look at Vera. Then a thought hit me, and I said, "I want to join forces with Yuri. Maybe by complementing Yuri's power, I would be able to see inside Vera without causing any harm."

Dusty didn't even need to think about that; he said yes without missing a beat. "I will talk to my grandmothers before I do anything. Plus, I need to talk to Yuri too," I added. My grandmothers had warned me before when I had told them I wanted to heal Vera. So, it was only natural to explain to them what I was planning. I didn't want to risk harming anyone.

It was after lunch that my father came to me and told me that my Uncle Andrei and Aunt Katarina would come by with Yuri. They, too, wanted the suffering to end. So I was pleasantly surprised when I saw my Uncle Vadim enter the house. He eyed me for quite some time, then he said, "You did well, Mitchell. You truly are a Balashov. I'm sorry that I ever doubted that."

I knew that he meant the healing of Ronan and capturing Igor and running defense for those who needed it. "Thank you, and I understand. I would have probably reacted the same. In the human world, the family would demand a DNA test. Apparently, Grandma Natalya didn't need one," I replied.

We walked side by side to the sunroom, and I filled him in about my mother's situation and that of Vera Reed. Uncle Vadim growled after hearing that Vera had tried to kill herself. My Aunt Katarina blinked profusely to keep the tears at bay. My mother had been one of her best friends. Now, she was back, but not quite. Yuri was eager to help, bless him.

Grandma Natalya had told me that it was okay to join Yuri to see if it was possible for me to help her. However, she cautioned me to keep a little distance and let Yuri lead the way. I had no problem with that. The main thing was that we would bring back my mother from wherever she was. My father needed his mate, and I needed my mother.

I had talked to Yuri about reading my mother and seeing if she was cursed with some kind of binding spell. Plus, reading Vera Reed, even though she wasn't a member of the Balashov Streak. Yuri had said that to him; it didn't matter. He saw people, not different species. I was so freaking proud of my nephew.

Chapter 33

We had planned a welcome home celebration for my mother and Grandpa Borya, but that would have to wait. First, we needed to undo whatever kept my mother from us. Yuri had examined my mother, or as he called it, he had read her. It turned out that there was, indeed, a dark binding spell that kept her imprisoned. That prevented my mother from connecting with the world. I wondered if, even though my mother seemed unresponsive, she understood what was said.

Right now, my mother seemed to be in some kind of catatonic state. So, we needed to find a way to remove the binding spell. But, to rid my mother of that damn spell wouldn't get easy. Grandma Natalya had written some pretty difficult spells these previous days. And, together with Grandma Anichka, she had made powerful potions to support the spells. However, now they had to rise to the challenge because this was dark magic that my grandmothers were up against.

Yuri's description had been perfectly clear, and that's why my grandmother knew that this was about dark magic. Igor must have forced a warlock into helping him to cast a spell of nonrecognition over my mother. So, both my grandmothers were working frantically on a counterspell and several potions to lift the curse, as they called it.

Grandma Natalya had explained to me that whenever a warlock casts a spell over a good person that it is considered a curse. So for good witches to undo a curse was very risky. Furthermore, Grandma Anichka had told me that witches had died in their effort to undo a curse. So, yes, it would get tricky.

I already told them that I would be there every step of the way; after all, it concerned my mother. There was something else that worried me. My mother's heartbeat was getting weaker. I didn't know what it meant, but I did know that it wasn't good. It could have to do with the curse. Her heartbeat was getting weaker ever since we had taken her from the Finch Place.

Grandma Anichka would assist Grandma Natalya in making the potions. I would help Grandma Natalya write a perfect spell, one that wouldn't put us in harm's way. But, of course, that meant that we had to come up with a spell that would prevent the actual spell from backfiring.

A spell that backfired was what caused the death of most witches who tried to lift a curse. Some thought that writing a counterspell was enough. Well, as you can guess, those poor witches didn't survive.

My grandmother had warned me that it could take days before the spell and the potion would be ready. After all, she didn't want to kill anyone, and she herself didn't want to die either.

Three days had gone by, and still no spell and no potion. I spend the days in my mother's room. She hadn't spoken, hadn't eaten, or drunk. Her heart was getting weaker and weaker, which drove me slowly insane with worry. My mother wasn't sitting in her chair anymore because she was too weak. She was in bed now all the time, sleeping, or I believed that she was. She lay in bed, eyes closed.

Then, a thought hit me, and I stormed out of the room. "Dad. Dad, where are you," I nearly yelled. "I'm in the sunroom. What's wrong?" He sounded alarmed because of my tone. "If they don't come up with a spell and potion today, then we need to bring mom back to the Finch Place," I said.

My father paled and looked confused. He shook his head as he said, "I don't think so, son." "Dad? Listen. When she was at Finch's Place, she appeared to be fine. But when we took her home, her heartbeat was getting weaker with every day that passed. I don't want her to die, dad," I pleaded.

My father considered me for a while. "I don't want her out of the house. This is the safest place for her to be. To bring her back to the Finch Place? I don't know, Mitchell. I honestly don't know," my father whispered. I understood him, I really did, but he didn't see the danger my mother was in right now. Because if Grandma Natalya would need a week to come up with a spell and a potion, my mother could die.

Dusty was with Vera, who had returned to The Hope Garden Psychiatric Institution. After all, she wasn't in danger anymore. Yuri had taken a look at Vera and had shaken his head. Vera was too fragile, and my Grandmothers had been right; Vera needed a lot more time to come to terms with the loss of her son. She was in a bad place right now because she didn't want to live anymore. Vera had given up, which was the worst-case scenario.

For as long as Vera was in this state of mind, no one could help her. Ronan did well; of that, I was glad. Him I had been able to help. When I received the healing gift, I had assumed that I could heal anyone. Well, I had been so very wrong. I hated that I couldn't help Vera. The woman still was suffering more than we could imagine. Vera wasn't the only one who suffered. No, Dusty was suffering just as much. He had to be the strong one because if he gave up, they would die together.

"Kotyonok? Did you hear any word I said?" I blinked a few times, turned, and saw my two Grandmothers standing in the doorway. "I'm sorry. Can you repeat that, please?" I asked. "We have the spells and special oil ready," Grandma Anichka said, smiling proudly. "That's great. What is it that you're going to use?" I questioned because I was curious.

"We have a potion that will protect us from backfiring, a protection potion if you will. Then, we have a cleansing potion because your mother's aura will need purification. After all, it's touched by dark magic," Grandma Natalya explained. "Then we wrote a spell to undo the curse, and that will bring, my daughter, your mother, back to us again. And finally, we created a blessing oil, which will strengthen the spells," Grandma Anichka said, and I could tell that she was eager to start. Well, so was I and everyone else.

Usually, a witch has to do some serious research before they are able to write a spell or brew a potion. However, Yuri had sped up the process by informing my grandmothers about what he had seen. Thus a description of the dark magic binding spell.

I was glad that we didn't need to bring my mother back to the Finch Place. My father told his mother and mother-in-law to start immediately with the incantation. Grandpa Borya did spend a lot of time in the garden with Grandpa Nicolay. They talk for hours about God knows what. Now, the two men had joined us in the room where my mother was. My father, Lamar, and my grandparents, all four of them, were present. Arkady was downstairs, as were several wolves and tigers.

We needed to wait for Yuri to arrive because only he could pinpoint the exact spot where we needed to concentrate on. So during the spell casting, Grandmother Natalya and I needed to point as much to the center of the spell as possible. So Yuri needed to visualize the spell, showing us where the center was. That way, the spell would be at its most powerful, and we would need all the power we could get.

"Where is he?" my father whispered impatiently while checking the time on his wristwatch. "I'm sure that they will be here any moment, dad," I soothed. My father didn't look convinced. Well, neither was I because too much had happened. I wouldn't be surprised if they got carjacked on their way to the mansion.

Chapter 34

"Are you ready? Kotyonok?" Grandma Natalya softly asked. I nodded. I was nervous because, hell, this was about bringing my mother back from the dark side. Yuri had pointed us where we needed to lay our focus. Uncle Andrei and Aunt Katarina had been stuck in traffic due to an accident that had happened. Now, we could finally free my mother of the chains that had held her for over twenty-six years. I wondered if she still was sane, once she would realize just how long she had been gone? Only time would tell.

I took the salt to draw a circle of protection around my mother. Grandma Natalya and I would be the only ones allowed into the circle. Next, I prepared the burner and the kettle.

My grandmother and I knew the spell by heart, so we didn't need a piece of paper to read from. We stepped into the circle I had drawn and looked at each other. This was the moment of truth. We would start with a protection spell, after that, the spell to lift the curse. Then, the cleansing spell, just to be sure that my mother's aura and soul were purified.

Last but not least, we would use the blessing oil that Grandma Anichka had made. Her mate had been rescued and at her side. And as of today, she would have her daughter back too. "Are you ready, kotyonok?" Grandma Natalya said. I nodded as I took her hand. Then we started casting the spell.

We are calm; we are strong
We can do no wrong
 We stand before you in the night
We are too strong to fight

Powers of night and day
We summon thee
Rosemary, lavender, and sage
Protect this place
Keep us safe

We burned the rosemary, lavender, and sage while saying the spell.

My mother didn't even stir. Was this normal? I didn't dare ask about that right now because we were in the middle of something dangerous. If this spell went wrong, we could die, and everyone in the room with us.

I removed the kettle and placed three black candles in a triangle. My grandmother nodded, letting me know to lighten the candles. So I did, then I took my place beside Grandma Natalya again. Now we began at the most dangerous part. If this went wrong, well, I won't go there because nothing would go wrong. We held hands and began chanting.

In our darkest hour
We call upon the sacred power
We stand tall, but not alone
We command the unseen to be shown
Break this spell break this curse
By candles three, by the end of this verse

Troubled soul with sleep unease
Remove the curse that cost this disease

Let her sleep for an hour more
So we can cleanse her inner core
Remove the curse now by the power of candles three
So mote it be.

This time, my mother began to stir, as if she was waking up, but then she went quiet again. It was an eerie sight. It must be because the spell would let her sleep for an hour more. We would need that time to rest for a while before casting the cleansing spell combined with the blessing oil.

"You did good, kotyonok. We're almost there," Grandma Natalya looked at Grandma Anichka; she softly said, "Today, you will get your daughter back." Grandma Anichka nodded because she was too emotional to answer. I was emotional too because I would get my mother back, finally. I've never even talked to the woman, and I longed for her touch. I had meditated before I was ready to cast the spells. My grandmother had warned me to be relaxed and only have positive thoughts. If I cast the curse lifting spell in anger, it could backfire.

My grandmother looked tired, but she smiled reassuringly when she eyed me. "Are you ready, kotyonok?" "Yes. Let's do this. Let's bring my mother back," I softly replied as I removed the three black candles and replaced them with two white ones and a blue one. We held hands once more, and my grandmother would rub the blessing oil onto my mother's forehead during the spell. The blessing oil contained sandalwood for cleaning, camphor for purification, orange for luck, patchouli for confidence, and olive oil. We looked at each other, and both nodded.

We call you spirits Sophie, Faith, and Grace

Cut all the cords from time and space
By the powers that be, by the candles times three
Clean this aura from all the debris
Remove its dark history
Fill her heart with love and light so pure
Let this for always be the cure

We chanted the spell three more times, and then it was
done. The tension in the room was palpable. I eyed my
grandmother, who smiled reassuringly. "We did well,
kotyonok," she softly said. I kissed her cheek, and then we
stepped out of the circle. We let the three candles burn and
the circle intact. "It's just a precaution," Grandmother
Natalya had assured me.

My father had gone very pale, and I could tell that
everything that had happened had taken its toll. Grandma
Natalya and I sat down, and Lamar handed us pomegranate
juice. "It has a lot of vitamins and antioxidants. Drink
everything," he urged. Grandma Natalya and I drained our
glasses. Lamar nodded approvingly.

About half an hour later, my mother began to stir. I
held my breath, as did my father. We stood side by side,
just outside the circle of salt. Then, she opened her eyes,
and I saw, for the first time, her true eye color. Before,
when she was under the dark binding spell, her eyes had
almost been colorless. Now, I was looking at the most
beautiful green eyes I had ever seen.

She looked at my father and seemed surprised to see
him. "Alexei? Is that you?" she paused, then added in a
whisper, "I don't understand." "Nadia? My love," my
father whispered as he stepped into the circle and knelt
beside the edge of the bed. He took his mate's hands in his
and gently kissed her.

For a short moment, they were whispering, and then my mother lifted her head and looked straight at me. "Mitchell?" she softly said as she held out her hand, reaching for me. "Yes, mother," I replied as I took her hand and sat on the edge of the bed. We hugged, and I was careful not to hold her too tight. I didn't know how fragile she was.

My grandparents joined us then as well. Grandma Anichka and Grandpa Borya were crying, just as my father and I were. I don't know for how long we had been sitting next to my mother's bed, but it was already dark outside. "Let's go downstairs, and we can slowly start to explain everything that had happened," my father suggested.

My mother considered my father for a short moment, then she looked at me and cocked her head. Suddenly her eyes filled with fear. "What is it, mother?" I softly asked, my voice full of concern. "Is this for real? Are you really here? Where am I? No, it's not real. You bastard, why are you torturing me like this? What have I done to you that you do this to me?" My mother went on and on, shocking the hell out of me.

"Shit," my father cursed, but before I asked what was going on, Grandmother Anichka pushed my father and me aside. She took my mother's face in her hands and forced her to look her in the eyes. "This is real. I'm real. Your father is real. Your mate is real, so is your son." The tone in which my grandma spoke was, well, odd. I'd never heard her use a tone as she had just used on my mother. Finally, my mother stopped rambling and eyed the room.

"I'm scared," my mother whispered as tears filled her eyes. She reached for my father and me. We hugged my mother tightly, my grandmother, my father, and me. "There's no need to be scared, my child. You're safe now," Grandma Anichka soothed.

We spend the evening talking, crying, and more talking. There was so much that my mother didn't know. She was relieved that Igor was dead so he couldn't come for her again. She had cried because she had missed twenty-six years of my life. She was glad that my father had never taken another partner. She couldn't remember much about her abduction.

Igor had told her that I had been stillborn and she was in danger. My mother had been grief-stricken; that was the only reason that Igor was able to take her. My mother was a strong shifter, even though she couldn't shift, like every female tiger shifter. She would have fought tooth and nail to keep Igor from taking her away from my father. I stared a lot at my mother; I looked a lot like her. I had my father's thick black hair, but my eyes, I had my mother's deep green eyes.

Chapter 35

"How are you doing, mother?" I asked as I kissed her cheek. She was in the garden where she had started growing herbs. My mother had told me that it made her feel at ease and that being in the garden cleared her head. A month had passed since she had been freed of the binding spell that had been cast by a warlock.

I hadn't told her, but I was searching for the bastard who had placed that spell. He would pay dearly once I got my hands on him. Lamar and my father knew because they were searching too. I knew that even if it took me ten years, I would find the one who was responsible. But for now, all we wanted was to enjoy the return of my mother and Grandpa Borya.

If we were human, I probably would have needed time with only my mother and father. But we weren't; we were shifters and thus one big family. So, everyone was in the house, and that night we celebrated the return of my mother and Grandfather Borya. Grandma Anichka had cried a lot the first hours, but now she was happy and wanted to celebrate that she had her mate back. The man had been missing for thirty years.

My mother had been soaking up all the information we gave her about the years she was, well, not with us. But, she was catching up quickly, and even though she had missed twenty-six years of my life, she wanted to focus on the future, and she showed so much strength.

My mother wanted to know everything that had happened in my life. And after I told her most of it, she said that she was very proud of me. I hadn't told her about the Jenkins that they had kicked me out because I was gay. That was something I would tell her later, much later.

Also, she wanted to visit the salon because she needed me to do her hair. As the evening progressed, it all felt so unreal. I mean, the woman was missing for twenty-six years. Then, my father was told that his mate had died giving birth. Now, after more than twenty-six years, she was home, safe and sound.

My mother proved to be a strong woman, she visited the salon, and I gave her a make-over at her request. It was her way of getting rid of the past, like another cleansing ritual. Now, a month after her homecoming, Grandma Anichka had offered to give her some memories of my years as a child. She had asked, and I had given permission. Grandma Natalya would, as a witch, make it happen. She said that it was the least she could do for my mother.

I wasn't entirely convinced because I didn't only have happy childhood memories. After all, the Jennings' had received a lot of money for adopting me. They had kicked me out of their house, and their life's when I told them that I was gay. So, no, I wasn't keen to share my childhood memories. Then again, she had a right to know. After I convinced her that it all had worked out for the best, she agreed to receive the memories.

After my mother had received the memories, she had cried for a long time. It was as if she had shed tears for those twenty-six years she had missed of my life. Then, after no tears were left, she had become the feisty woman

my father had told me about. But, as I said before, my
mother proved to be a strong woman. My parents still
spend a lot of time in the garden, talking, cuddling, and
well, you can guess the rest.

I looked around and sighed in contentment. My family
was complete; Grandpa Borya and my mother were
rescued. My friends were present as well. Liam had
accepted Eric as his mate, and they looked very happy
together. Felix, the hyena who had asked and was granted
sanctuary, had mated Dimitri Balashov, my uncle.

Secing my father so happy warmed my heart every
time. It was the same with my grandparents. All our
enemies were dead, which meant that we were safe. It also
meant that we could go on with our lives. I resumed
working at my salon, and Lamar was investigating the
disappearance of an older couple. My father spent all his
time with my mother, as was expected. Grandma Anichka
spent a lot of time with Grandpa Borya and, of course, my
mother. After all, she was their daughter.

My mother wasn't really amazed when I told her about
my second form. She told me that she had seen me, in my
second form, even before I was born. This was odd, but
nothing about my family was normal.

My mother was back home for a month now, and she
was getting restless. We had talked about starting her own
business. I told her that a few doors to the left of The
Cutting Edge Hair Salon, a small building was for sale. I
knew there had been a shoe store in it.

It turned out that my mother was very enterprising.
"I'll start a beauty salon where people can get their nails
done and can get a mani-pedi and facials. You know, the

usual," she had said. And by her expression, she was dead serious. I thought that it was a brilliant idea. My father didn't like it one bit. He was overprotective when it came to my mother, and I couldn't blame him. However, I told him not to suffocate her because that wouldn't be good. My mother, like any other person, needed room to breathe.

Even though it was difficult for him to do so, he encouraged her to start her beauty salon by the small building. But, my father had insisted that there would be bodyguards. Thank God my mother hadn't protested; she, too, understood. Later, she confided that she liked that bodyguards would keep her safe.

Even though she was feisty, my mother was still reeling from twenty-six years of imprisonment. She had refused to be a victim, and that's why she wanted, no needed, something to call her own. The beauty salon was something that she could control; it was precisely what she needed.

Also, my mother's memory slowly returned, which meant that in time she would recall every single day of those twenty-six years of hell. I didn't know what to think of that. Maybe we should come up with some kind of spell to prevent those memories from surfacing? My mother had shut me down hard when I suggested it. She told me that it was part of her life and that she would deal with it.

It was good to see that Felix and Dimitri had mated and seemed happy with each other. The way Dimitri looked at Felix said it all. The man was smitten, he adored Felix, and the hyena reveled in the attention he got from the big strong tiger. Alyona had left Serigala Valley, but she had sworn to get revenge. Well, let her try, the bitch.

Liam was happy, and that Igor and the Karr brothers were dead was the icing on the mating cake, as he put it.

That left Ralph, he was the only one of my friends who still was single, but he didn't seem to mind. He once had told me that he was happy with his life at it was. I believed him at that moment, but he would change his mind if the right person crossed his path. He had laughed when I had told him that. Well, we would see.

For a while, life seemed perfect. However, if something sounds too good to be true, it mostly is. Arden, Felix's friend, was miserable; the hyena seemed depressed. I hadn't noticed before because, with all that was going on, Arden had slipped my attention. Now that things had calmed down, I noticed that he didn't laugh, didn't have fun. What was worse, the man didn't participate anymore. He had retreated more and more until the day he didn't even leave his room anymore. So, I was concerned and decided to look in on him.

I went upstairs to where Arden had his room and softly knocked. "Come in," a soft voice said. The room was dark, even though the sun was shining brightly. "Hey, Arden." The hyena looked up, and seeing the sad expression in his eyes nearly broke my heart."Is it alright if I sit down?" I asked in a gentle tone. Arden nodded. "Sure, it's your house. You don't need to ask permission," he reluctantly replied.

I admit that his answer caught me a bit off guard. "No, Arden. This is your room, and you decide what happens in here," I assured him. "You're not happy, I can tell. Do you want to tell me what's wrong?" I carefully inquired.

Arden was silent for a long time, as if he was searching for the words or if he would confide in me at all. I hoped he would trust me enough to tell me what was bothering him. Arden sighed deeply, and he blinked profusely to keep the tears at bay. I knew from Felix that Titus hadn't tolerated if a hyena showed emotions.

I waited patiently, but when Arden stayed silent, I said, "I know how it was with your former pack. We do things differently here. For example, it's okay to show feelings, to let us know what it is that you want, or need."

Arden lifted his head, his look guarded; he softly said, "My mate, I don't know where she is. She should have called me by now because she wanted away from the clan as well." I didn't even know that Arden had a mate. Come to think of it; I didn't know anything about Arden. My only excuse was that there had been a lot going on.

"Did you try and call her?" "Yes, but it goes straight to voicemail," Arden softly replied. "What is her name so that I can organize a search," I offered because mates were precious. Well, love was precious. "I don't know if you want to help me find her if you know who she is," Arden softly said.

I frowned; it was obvious that Arden had no idea how things were in the Balashov Streak or the McLaughlin Pack. "Well, only one way to find out," I said. Arden looked me straight in the eyes. "Paulina Karr," he whispered. That had me off guard. "Is she family of Titus Karr?" I questioned because my curiosity was aroused. "Yes, she's his daughter," Arden replied. "It doesn't matter whose daughter she is. Paulina is your mate, and we will find her," I promised.

So, my to-do list grew longer and longer. First, find
Paulina Karr, so Arden could reunite with his mate because
mates shouldn't be separated. Then, we needed to find the
warlock who had helped Igor cast the spell that would bind
my mother. She had been taken from her newborn child
and her mate, my father. My mother had missed the first
twenty-six of my life. Not to mention the suffering my
father had endured, thinking all those years that his mate
was dead. Well, I wouldn't rest until he was dead.

That same warlock had a hand in the attempted murder
of Felix by conjuring this thick gray kind of mist. And he
probably was the same warlock who helped enlarge Titus
and Igor's animals. So, he was high on my list.

And last but not least, Alyona Barinov, Dimitri's ex.
She had poisoned Gregor, Dimitri's best friend, and why?
Because of the money. Gregor was human, and he had
cancer, which was cost by Alyona. God only knew what
she had used to poison the poor man with.

Dimitri would inherit a few million dollars, and
Alyona wanted that money. So she had planned to marry
Dimitri, then wait until Gregor died, and Dimitri would get
his millions. She then would hire someone to kill Dimitri,
and then Alyona would inherit a lot of money.

I hoped that I was wrong, but my gut feeling told me
that trouble was lurking around the corner.

To be continued

About the Author

I always find it challenging to write something about myself, but here it goes.

I'm fifty-something, and I started on my first book in 2012. Some people call me a late bloomer, and I guess that I am. I married my wonderful hubby when I was thirty-three years. According to my mother, it took me too long to get married and finally settle down. I think that it was just the right time. I don't have kids. I have two dogs who are my life.

I'm a dreamer, always have been, always will be. I believe in true love and romance. I believe in people.
I live in a small village because I love peace and quiet. I love camping, especially if it's in Italy. If I'm not working on a story, I spend time with my dogs.

Other work of Haley Langwood

Julian - Grapevines & Skyscrapers Book 1
Reunited - Grapevines & Skyscrapers Book 2
Weddingbells - & Skyscrapers Book 3

Jory's Destiny - The Wentworth Pack Book 1
Family Matters - The Wentworth Pack Book 2
Insanity - The Wentworth Pack Book 3
Children of the Gods - The Wentworth Pack Book 4

Guardian Angels

Christmas Miracles - A Voice from Heaven

Serigala Valley

Rescues – Dutch and English Edition
Rescues 02 Emma a Journey to Happiness

Links

https://haleylangwood.wixsite.com/mijnsite

https://www.facebook.com/HaleyLangwoodwriter/